Breadline Blue

LORNA MACDONALD CZARNOTA

To Fred —
Love, Lorna
2020

LITTLE CREEK BOOKS
A division of Jan-Carol Publishing, Inc.
Johnson City, TN

LITTLE CREEK BOOKS
A division of Jan-Carol Publishing, Inc.
Johnson City, TN

Breadline Blue

LORNA MACDONALD CZARNOTA

Published February 2013

ISBN: 978-1-939289-11-7
Library of Congress Control Number: 2013902798

You may contact the publisher:
Jan-Carol Publishing, Inc.
PO Box 701
Johnson City, TN 37605
E-mail: publisher@jancarolpublishing.com
www.jancarolpublishing.com

To my parents, David and Mary MacDonald
You would have loved this one!
Thank you for giving me the love of
reading and learning.

Acknowledgments

Thank you to the following people, without whom this book would not be possible.

To my publisher, Janie Jessee, editor, Tammy Robinson Smith and graphic designer, Tara Sizemore. Thank you for seeing a good story in *Breadline Blue.*

To my initial readers, Northern Adams, Susanna Connelly Holstein and Jim Phitzer, for checking the Appalachian voice and other aspects of this story.

To Laura Parker and Miriam Nadel for your advice on period Jewish words and ideas. Also to Holly Gold, Bill Allen and Michelle Wheeler for your historical input.

To musician and friend Tom Naples, for your knowledge on this history, especially the hobo lifestyle.

To Kerri Dooley Bahner, proprietress of Kinfolk Restaurant in Selinsgrove, Pa, you are the best.

To Nick Zmijewski curator of the Pennsylvania Railroad Museum, who helped with line schedules and train details.

And last but not least, to Thomas Heim, you are more than a reader, you are my inspiration and go-to guy.

Dear Reader,

The story of *Breadline Blue* is more than the story of one boy. It is the story of a nation, of young people and their families, struggling to make sense of difficult times, and overcoming the odds. I chose to tell this story from the perspective and in the dialect of the main character, William Saxton. Now you can take the adventure with him, and see the world as he does, through the eyes of a poor Appalachian farm boy, during the Great Depression.

The Great Depression was an era in this country's history that truly tested the morals and standards by which people lived. Based on research of the period and events, this story is factual in every way, except that I created the characters. I've also done tribute to several friends, colleagues and family members. I hope you enjoy trying to figure out who they are.

The towns and cities in this tale are real, but I took liberties in describing some of them, especially in my portrayal of Selinsgrove, Pennsylvania. I attempted to paint as true a picture of small-town America as possible, using maps from the Internet, a visit to the town, and combining that information with other small towns I have been to in my travels.

The songs included in this story are songs from the era, many of which I sang while performing with a period string band. The title of this book was inspired by one of those songs.

The events in this story aren't all pretty and sweet. Many children who ran away from home and rode the rails, were used and abused as is Blue. And riding the rails was just as dangerous as this story suggests. Many young people lost their lives.

Perhaps, most exciting for me, as the author, was allowing this story to unfold naturally, as it progressed. I knew who was going where and why. I had no idea what Blue would do or find along the way. I let "him" tell me that. Discovering Eleanor Roosevelt's diary online was also a treasure. It helped me figure out the dates of Blue's travels and exactly where Mrs. Roosevelt would be when he arrived in Washington. The answer was a surprise, even to me!

I hope you enjoy this journey of self-discovery with *Breadline Blue.*

The Leaving

I stood lookin' at the house for a long time. It hadn't changed, still a small white-washed farmhouse about three miles outside town. Had I expected it to change as much as I had? I don't know, but I do know, I ain't never been so scared in all my days, not even with what I seen and done. I had no idea what Mama would say or if she would even recognize me. I was taller by a bit, thinner, and wearing new clothes. Would she want me home? I had left her with all the cares of our family, after all.

"Son," said the policeman standin' behind me. "If you don't get yourself up to the door, I'm gonna have to break orders and take you myself."

"Yessir," I mumbled. Then I heard Mama's voice. She must have come to the door and I didn't even see her.

"Billy!" She shouted, already half way cross the yard. "Billy is that you! Thanks be."

She stopped for a moment and looked up at heaven when she said that, but the rest of her words was cut off by a flow of tears as she swept me into her large warm arms. And me, a growed man of seventeen, I just bawled like a baby.

It was days and days before I could tell Mama everything about my adventure.

June 17, 1937

It was the whistle again, that lonesome far away WHOOOOOOOO and the CLATTERY CLAT of the train. It was my lullaby. It sung me to sleep deep in the night and put dreams in my head. Dreams of things I could never have and didn't really want, like a fine house and fancy clothes, and a bicycle. Only, I really did want the bicycle, just never said so.

Every single night for a year and a half that train come when I needed it and that cool June night in 1937 was no different. I wasn't sleeping too good most nights. I guess it was true for so many of us poor folk. People was either too hungry to sleep or just too tired. I reckon it sounds funny but when a man is so tired and weary, worrying about how he might feed his family or whether he'll have a job next day, his soul wears out and sleep just don't come. Well anyway, that's what Pa used to say.

My train come around midnight, about the time my eyes started to droop. I recall I was just on the edge of one of them pretty dreams when the sawing started, a low rumble at first, back and forth like a man pulling his saw across a board, but then it got louder. It became more of a buzz saw, like the ones at the mill my pa used to work at. Only Pa didn't work no more as he was too sick in his lungs. The doctor called it "new-moania" or something like that. Pa? Yes, it was Pa and not a saw I was hearing. I sat bolt upright in my bed. Pa was coughing again.

I went to the bedroom door where I seen Mama sitting up in bed rapping on Pa's back and Pa all bent over hacking up his lungs. Mama give me a stern look, but I seen the worry behind her eyes, and I seen her hands. They was all red and sore again from doing other folk's laundry and mending. Mama had to work so we had enough to eat. I did what I could with odd chores when I could find them in town. I was in school when I wasn't working and fishing at the river more than I was at school, I guess. Sitting at a desk doing numbers and alphabet was next to impossible with my mind wandering all the time.

"You get yerself back to bed, Billy. Ain't nothin' you can do here."

Mama's voice broke into my thoughts. I started to complain, but I knew she was right. I wanted to help. I wanted to help so bad it hurt. I was sixteen years old and able, but she was right. Doc said there was nothing anybody could do, Pa was dying and we both knew it. Nothing on this earth could change Pa's fate, not even the letter I wrote to Mrs. Roosevelt at the White House.

She's the President's wife you know and sure sounded like a nice woman from what they said on the radio, so I took a chance. I reckon she got plenty of letters, but not from kids like me. I still remember what I wrote.

Dear Mrs. Roosevelt:

My name is Billy, but folks mostly call me Blue cause my eyes is so blue in color. But that's not why I'm writing. I'm writing to say thank you because you and Mr. Roosevelt are trying so hard to make things better for folks, and to ask you for a favor. I reckon you are a mighty busy lady, but I thought you could take some time to say a prayer for my Pa who's really sick and maybe dying. Mama works hard to buy food but we don't get much and the doctor says he can't help my Pa. If you ever have any food left over in the kitchen you don't need, I wonder if you could send some to my pa, especially chicken soup. I reckon your soup is much thicker than ours since it probably has chicken in it and I think it would help. And, if you have a dress you don't need no more, maybe you could send that for my ma. I don't need nothing for myself right now.

Billy

I don't know what I was thinking, writing to such a busy lady. She never wrote back and watching my Pa dying and Mama working herself to the bone was breaking my heart. I made up my mind. One way or another I was going to take the train. Either it would take me to sleep or I would take it to Washington. I didn't sleep all night.

June 18, 1937

The next morning there was one of those lonesome dreary rains, the kind that makes the sky so gray and heavy not even the birds wanna sing. On those days, you could feel the whole world weighing down on your back. Usually Mama was up at the crack of dawn, but the night with Pa had taken its toll and even she didn't stir.

It was the last day of school before summer but I couldn't wait no more. I buttoned my old work shirt, pulled my old overall straps up over my shoulders and slipped my feet into my going-to-church shoes. I only had one pair. Most times we all just went barefoot. Mama made me put those shoes neat under the bed and said "Don't know when we'll get new ones Billy, so you set those aside for Sundays. Can't go to the Lord's house with bare feet and bare heads." I remember watching her put her favorite, and only, straw hat up on the shelf and cover it with an old towel. She only wore that hat on Sundays, just like I wore my shoes. I always thought it looked odd, her wearing a tattered dress with a like-new hat. But she always looked pretty to me, even beyond the grey hairs starting on her head.

Ma told me she married Pa when she was seventeen. They had my brother a year later and then me the year after. I reckon plenty of folks married young and started families right away, though they didn't talk much about it. Mama probably wouldn't have talked about it neither, 'cept I asked. I was always asking things. Wanted to know where we come from, when I was born, why my brother Richie died. Mama said he took the fever at age three and I was too young to remember. She said they was so scared I'd get sick too, only "Praise the Lord," Mama said. "He saw to spare you."

One Sunday, after church when I was seven years old, Mama and Pa took me to the cemetery. They said it was time to show me where my brother was sleeping in eternal peace. It was mighty strange for me. I remember them pointing to a headstone that read Richard Saxton and saying he was my Granddaddy.

"How come it ain't my brother, his name is Richie?" I asked.

"Your brother was named after Pa's daddy," Mama explained. She always did most of the explaining. Pa never was big on words, but I turned to him then.

"Pa, how come you don't talk about your Pa? How come there ain't no headstone for Richie? Where's your Ma?"

He didn't say nothing. Mama stepped in as she usually did. "Sometimes folks can't put a headstone, Billy. They're very expensive you know. We will someday."

Ma and Pa never answered the rest of my questions, and I didn't push them.

***

I heard Mama stir and knew if I was gonna do it, leave and all, I had better get a move on. I decided to take my shoes off so they wouldn't make noise on the wood floor. I tied the laces together and threw the pair over my shoulder. I tiptoed to the kitchen.

I laid my old hankie out on the table and took a chunk of bread out of the tin box and a couple hard-boiled eggs from the icebox. I felt a little guilty about taking the food but I needed something to get me on my way. I knew Mama had to sew all day to trade for those eggs. Somehow I thought she'd understand when I come home with a whole kettle of soup from Washington.

The bedroom door creaked open and I crumpled up the hankie and stuffed it in my big ole pockets. I just made it out the back door and grabbed my fishing pole when Mama come to the kitchen. I took off in a run down over the yard and through the broken fence at the back before she could see me. I don't know what happened in the house after that. All I knew was my feet kept a running until I come to the river and I never looked back.

***

I use the words "my train" loosely of course. It wasn't in my plans to wait until midnight to "hop the rails." That's what the fellas at the barbershop called it. I didn't get my hair cut there. Mama just stuck the bowl on my head and give me a free haircut, but I spent lots of time listening to the old men tell stories.

"My train" coulda been any train between now and tomorrow but I pretty much knew which one I wanted. Being my first time, I didn't want to wait til dark. I come down to that fishing spot enough to know there would be an eastbound-train come by the bridge on the other side of the river at about eleven, but it wouldn't be for a couple hours. There was just enough time to get in some fishing and maybe cook it up for breakfast.

The rain held off until I caught my first fish, then it commenced to being a drencher. Looked like I wasn't gonna roast my fish after all, unless I did it under the bridge, which I thought might be best. The rain and the bridge would keep folks from seeing me. And with the rain coming down as it was, I was pretty certain Mama wouldn't be out looking for me. Besides, it was Friday and as far as she knew, I mighta left early for school. Still, there was no reason to chance it. She might be happy when I come home with whatever Mrs. Roosevelt saw fit to give me, but she wasn't about to let me go tramping or rambling or whatever she'd call it. No sir, and I didn't have no fondness for the strap. That was usually Pa's job, giving me the strap when I done wrong, but it was Mama who scared me most right then. Pa was too sick to do the whipping and Mama had no experience. She never raised a hand to me in all my days and I guessed she wouldn't do it none too well, even if she had a mind to on that day.

I run on downstream until I got to the bridge, then crossed over to the rail side of the river. The road ran north and south through town and out past our place before turning east to the next town. The railroad ran east and west and crossed over the road just a few yards from the bridge. Pa always said it was poor planning to put the two so close together, but that day I was thinking it a blessing. Oh, I could have waited at the water tank closer to town, but then I'd be seen for sure. This way, the train would already have been through town and on its way. It always slowed down at the crossing. I stood and watched it many times and I knew just what I was gonna do. I stood there in the rain for a few minutes with the picture in my head. Wait til the train starts up, let five cars pass, start running long side and hop on the next boxcar. If I didn't let enough cars go by before jumping, the engineer might see me, or worse, I might be spotted by the rail police. They real police at all, but vigilante men hired by the railroad to keep vagrants, migrants, and other ne'er-do-wells from riding without a ticket. I didn't want to get caught and if I waited too long, then the train would be going too fast. I had to time it just right.

I was standing there thinking it out, when a hand pressed into my arm and nearly sent me flying in fright. I woulda screamed too, but another hand come up hurriedly and shot over my mouth.

"Boy," said a voice. I was thinking police or truant officer and the end of my journey before it even started. "You better not stand out there and get caught because they'll get us both."

Next thing I know, I was pulled back under the bridge just at the waters' edge and spun around. The whole thing took the breath outta me.

It wasn't a long time he held me there, but long enough for me to take him in. The face looking back at me was a man in his early thirties with a grizzled beard and dirt smearing his cheeks. His hair was cropped short and tucked under a newsboy cap. He wore a pair of overalls like my own and a pair of old tennis shoes.

"I won't hurt you. Just don't scream or run when I let go. All right now?"

His voice wasn't mean.

I nodded best I could under his grip. He had my one arm pulled back and I felt it might snap if I struggled.

"Promise?"

I nodded again and he left me free. I didn't know what to say. He spoke first.

"What's your name, son?"

"Billy. But my friends call me Blue."

"Am I a friend, Billy?"

"Well, I don't know you do I? But as long as you don't truss me up again, I reckon you can call me Blue." It didn't matter to me what he called me cause I wasn't ever gonna see him after that day. "Why did you go and pull me down here? I was thinking about how I was gonna hop the train. What's your name?"

"Let's just say my friends call me Pete. I pulled you down here because by the look of you you're a runaway. Am I right?"

I nodded again. "So what?"

"So, I been there a time or two myself and if you don't want to be caught and sent back, you better stay out of sight until you hear the whistle," He smiled and then let out a long lonesome WOOOO that sounded just like a train. "Even then, I don't advise you to be heading out until the first couple cars go by. This bridge is good cover and besides, why get wet when you don't need to?"

It was too late. I was already soaked through and what's more, when he grabbed me, he tore my flimsy shirt, and now my arms gone all goose pimply.

"Don't you have another shirt with you?" he asked looking me over.

I reckon it was plain to see I didn't even have a bag, in fact my fishing pole and fish was still lying out in the rain. I hung my head, kinda ashamed I hadn't thought about a change of clothes or jacket for that matter. The weather was getting warmer every day and June-time in the Appalachians of Pennsylvania was usually just right for no shirt, only after the day warmed. Right now, it was still chilly and the rain didn't help.

"Well?"

"No sir," don't know why I called him "sir" neither. Something in his voice or his face seemed to want respect.

"Well, then, I guess you better have one of mine."

Pete reached behind a fallen tree branch that had apparently washed up on the bank and fetched up a satchel. He fumbled through it and come out with a blue and white checked shirt, a little large for me, but not too big. I caught it as he tossed it over.

"You put that on, now. It'll warm you."

"Mister, I can't take no handout and besides you might need this here shirt. It don't have no holes or nothing."

I thought of Mama mending clothes for other folks. With the price of a shirt these days, if somebody saw to mending it, then it was dearly bought.

"You take it, son. I got another. You aren't prepared for this, you know, but stick with me awhile. You'll learn."

I guess I looked reluctant but he urged me on.

"Go on now, put it on before you catch your death of pneumonia."

I was back at the farm again. "New-moania." That's what Pa had. No, I couldn't get sick because who would take care of my folks then? No sir. I put on the shirt and it did me for a long time after. Looked might smart with my blue eyes too, that's what folks would say, "Sets off them baby blues."

Pete and me gathered up enough dry wood from under the bridge to cook up the fish. He had some matches and a frying pan. I had my old penknife. I reckon Pete had a better one but he didn't say so. He just let me do it like I would have without him. Nothing tastes better than a fish you caught with your own hands and that's the truth. At least for a little while I forgot the rain and Pa, even would have forgot the train. We just got done eating when we heard the first whistle some ways off.

"You stay close now," said Pete. "If we get split up, take the first car you can. Don't try to reach me. I'll find you. Promise?"

Pete sure made me feel better. I promised and we grabbed up our stuff. He had to leave the pan behind as it was still too hot to handle, but we'd find another one on down the road. Fact is, plenty of folks was traveling the trains and I'd soon find out folks left things behind for the next man to use.

***

We stayed low at the edge of the bridge until we seen the engine and a couple cars pull slowly by. Once the engine passed, the train give out another long low whistle.

"That's it!" Pete shouted. "He'll be speeding up. Let's go!"

Off Pete went running with his head down, back toward the rear of the train and me following right on his heels. *One car, two cars, three cars, four.* I counted them in my head like a nursery rhyme we learned when I was a baby. I watched Pete like a hawk watching prey. Something told me I'd need to know what to do someday if I found myself without him..

As the train started taking on speed, Pete threw his pack into an open car and grabbed onto the ladder. He swung his left leg up over the edge and threw himself just like his satchel. I couldn'ta been more than two feet behind him, right on his heels. Pete held out his hand and I took hold of his wrist and with his other hand on my wrist I was hauled up and in just as the train gained more speed. I was onboard and we was on our way. I let loose my breath. Reckon I'd been holding it the whole time. I pulled a long fresh breath of dusty air and choked. Pete give me a slap on the back.

"Gonna be just fine," he said. "Just take your ease for now."

As I leaned for the first time against the boarded sides of the train car I felt my belly fill with a mix of excitement and uncertainty, like the feeling you get right before a foot race or a spelling bee.

Life was changed right then and for always. Somehow I knew it, and it wasn't too long before the rails humming beneath my bones and the car rocking back and forth put me to sleep. I dreamed of Mama's arms and her old rocking chair.

A New Friend

Pete turned out to be a pretty interesting guy, once I got past the fright of him sneaking up on me at the bridge. He knew loads about the world; said he had traveled plenty when he was working. I asked what happened to his job and he said he was like everybody else—down on his luck.

You know, it's a funny thing how you can look at a man and tell a lot about him even before he says anything. I learned that from Pa. He always said, "Look at a man's hands and how he holds himself, and if he looks you in the eye." Well, Pete's hands was dirty, I reckon cuz it's just hard keeping clean while riding the rails, but they didn't have the same deep calluses as Pa's. They was almost smooth. And well, I reckon I've seen plenty of downtrodden men and they always walks with a bit of a hunch in their shoulders, like they was afraid to look and see God looking back at 'em.

Pete, he always sat with what Mama called good posture. She was always making me sit up straight with my shoulders back. Pa would add, "Tuck that chin in, Son. Don't want folks to think you got yer nose in the air."

Pa had been in the Army so the chin tuck-shoulders back business was right important to him. Pete had an air about him. He walked proud and confident. I liked that about him, and the fact he looked me in the eye when he talked.

"A man can't bury the truth if he is looking you in the eye," Pa said.

So I knew Pete was a cut above, I just didn't know how much above at the time. Whenever we wasn't just sitting in the car, I was studying Pete. Yep, he sure had good posture and good manners. Mama woulda liked him.

***

We rode all day the first day out with me sleeping much of the way. Pete give me a shoulder shake and asked if I was doing all right. I guess some boys get a little queasy first time, but I said I was doing just fine, which I was. I rubbed the sleep from my eyes and through the open boxcar door I seen it was almost dark. I guess I was so plain tuckered I musta slept right through the water stops for the train's steam engines.

Shadows flew past the train. It was that twilight grey when everything has a lazy glow and seems to say, "Time to call it a day." That's when the boys usually come in from the fields for supper. I had a little guilty pang, realizing I had slept during working time. It didn't feel quite right, but what else was there to do?

I started thinking about home. I reckoned Mama was feeding Pa just about then. I really prayed hard she was taking time to feed herself too. She was the kind of woman to forget herself more than I cared for.

"What time you reckon it is, Pete?" I asked.

I got one of my first Pete surprises—well maybe the second one because the shirt he give me sure was a nice one. Pete reached his two fingers into his bib-pocket and took out something round and flat. It was a pocket watch. A man with dirty hands in bib-overalls taking out what seemed to be a shiny pocket watch was surely not what you would expect.

"That's a mighty fine thing you got," I said.

"Yep, a solid gold remnant of the past. It's going on seven."

"What?"

"You asked the time. It's going on seven."

"No, Pete, I mean what you said, something about the past."

He handed that fine timepiece over to me.

"Take a look," Pete said.

My first inclination was to look at the watch face of course. The numbers was strange. A lesson from school crept into my head—Roman numerals. It always amazes me, what things I recall and the things I don't. I took Pete's word for the time because while I knew they was Roman, I just couldn't remember the one from the seven or anything else for that matter. I started to hand it back.

"Go ahead, son. Turn it over."

I closed the lid and flipped the watch over on its back. There was writing on it. "Veni vidi vici."

Yeah, I know I said I skipped school plenty but I'm a fair reader, and Mama could read and she was, in no uncertain terms, all for reading. We didn't have money for books of our own, except the Bible of course, and Mama made sure I read from it. But I just couldn't make out the words, just like I couldn't tell the Roman numbers.

"That's an inscription," Pete told me.

"Well, I don't speak no inscription," I said and Pete laughed.

"No, son, an inscription isn't a language. It's a phrase or sentiment. Some words saying who the watch is for or why it was given."

"Well, what's it say?"

Pete was silent for a moment. "You know, it really doesn't matter what it says."

He clammed up but like I said, I always ask questions and I wanted to know. Pete reached out to take the watch but I pulled it back.

"Nope. You give me a scare at the bridge, I don't know you, so I want to know what it says. Did you steal it or something?"

Pete laughed again. "No, it isn't stolen. It's mine. The words say 'veni, vidi, vici'. It means, I came, I saw, I conquered."

"Are you sure you didn't take this from somebody?" I asked again, not quite believing Pete could have been so important as all that. I mean, to look at him in overalls, dirt, worn out tennis shoes; you never woulda guessed he could own it. Then I got to thinking about how he sat up straight and spoke so well.

He looked me straight in the eye and said again "No, it's mine."

I let out a low long whistle. "Geez," was all I could say. I was traveling with a gosh-darn Swell or something. Then I wondered what his kind was doing riding in a boxcar with the likes of me? And how come he was so nice and all? The fellas at the barbershop always said the Swells was uppity and wouldn't give you the time of day, but there was Pete just give me the time of day. The questions I wanted to ask got stuck in my craw. Reckon they weren't polite.

Didn't have much time to think about my decision as the sickening loud squeal of the train wheels on the rails shook me out of my thoughts. I watched as Pete jumped suddenly to his feet and peered out the open boxcar door.

"Damn it," I heard him say under his breath. Instinctively, Pete reached for his satchel and with the other hand, slowly slid the door partway closed until the opening was just big enough for a man to squeeze through.

"What's wrong Pete?" I asked, following his lead and getting to my feet. I looked just over his right shoulder far enough to see down the tracks in front of us as the train come to a halt. All I could see was shadows flying from boxcars ahead. I looked back and seen a few more shadows from behind. Then I saw the torches moving down the tracks in our direction. Every now and then they stopped in front of a car and I heard the door creak open. That's when I heard a barking dog.

"Bulls!" Pete shouted. "The railroad vigilante." I knew enough to know it weren't good. Pete give a look and a nod, "Run that way," he pointed away from the train "and don't stop running. I'll keep up. Now go!"

I hesitated and Pete shoved me from behind. Did you ever get pushed with one foot already in the air? It's like flying for a minute and then you realize you ain't got wings. I soared maybe five feet over the tracks and down the low cinder embankment, but unlike a cat I didn't land on my feet. About midway I felt my balance shift and my feet curled up behind me while the rest of me did a nosedive forward. I landed with my hands outstretched in front, natural instinct-like. I felt a quick searing pain on my right palm before my feet caught up with the rest of me and I heard a dog. "Barroooo." One of them bloodhounds! Something in my legs took over and my head never touched the ground, nor did my feet I think. "Run!" was all I heard from behind and I could tell Pete was at my tail.

I wasn't aware until then but I musta put my shoes on while Pete was first looking out the boxcar door, only I didn't have time to tie the laces. My left foot come down on the lace of my right shoe about then and I tumbled again. This time my landing was softer—not in the cinders, but into some scrub brush.

"Ugh," somebody grunted as I landed flat over him.

Pete seen our tangled bodies and sort of did a leap over us to the other side.

"Shh, hush up," the man said pushing me off to one side. He sat up and commenced to watchin' through the bushes. Seemed like he didn't much care what we did and I reckon it made sense. By what I could see in the dark, he was like us—a refugee from the train. I heard the old hound dog barking off in the distance. I could tell he turned off away from us.

"They went on by," he finally said. "Leastwise, some of them. The rest is by the train with some they caught, so keep it down."

When he spoke, I saw the shadowy gap where his front tooth used to be. He held out a grubby hand and whispered, "Mack's the name."

When I didn't take his hand, he pulled it back and rubbed some of the dirt off on his trousers, then held his hand out again.

"Blue," I said.

He looked at my traveling companion who nodded and said "Pete."

"That was mighty close. They got those Bulls all up and down this line. Railroad is really cracking down on freeloaders."

Pete spoke up. "What do you think we should do? You planning to reboard?"

"Not me," Mack said. "No sir, I think it'd be best to lay low for the night and see what comes by in the morning. Where you headin'?"

Pete shrugged. "I'm always heading whichever way the train is going I guess. How about you?"

Mack thought for a minute and then said, "Lookin' for work in the next town."

Then they both looked at me. I hadn't said nothing yet and hadn't even told Pete nothing.

I wondered if I should say where I was headed as well, and guessed it wouldn't hurt none. I shrugged. "D.C. I reckon."

Pete's eyes narrowed. I seen that look before. Mama made that face when she looked over my schoolwork sometimes.

"Billy, don't you know how much change you would get from one dollar if you bought a ball for one dime?"

"No, Mama, I ain't never had a dollar."

"You have never, Billy. Not ain't."

"Yes, Mama."

Then she took out some sewing buttons and a patch of cloth from her basket.

"Say this is your dollar." She held up the cloth. "There are ten dimes in one dollar, Billy. Count them out."

I counted the buttons, "One, two, three . . ."

When I had ten counted out, Mama said, "Now you count by tens like this. Ten, twenty, thirty, forty, fifty."

I counted out the rest following her lead. Mama told me to take away one dime, one button.

"Now, that pays for your ball, Billy. How much is left?"

Mama smiled mighty pretty and proud when I counted the rest in my head and shouted, "Ninety! Ninety cents in change, Mama."

"Billy?" It was Pete calling me back to the field by the tracks. "Why Washington?"

"Oh, I don't know. Thought I might find some help there."

Mack almost choked when I said it.

"Lord alive, kid, the folks in Washington don't give a damn about you or me. All they care about is getting their votes. You want to get help, you better get it yourself. Hell, you'd be better off with the Big Rock Candy Mountain."

He give Pete an elbow but Pete only scowled. I think it made me kinda mad. I ain't sure if it was the way he said it, or if it was because Mrs. Roosevelt was a nice lady, or because it went against the very reason I run away. I suppose I didn't answer too kindly.

"Well, I don't suppose you know everything there is to know and you sure as heck don't know me."

"Whoa, kid, I didn't mean nothing. Don't get your britches in a twist. If we end up traveling together, we gotta git along, at least where it matters."

Pete winked at me and put a hand on my shoulder. The weight of his hand just said it'll be okay.

"Look, I think it's safe to say once the train moves off, we can start a fire and stay here the night. You in?" Mack asked.

Pete deferred to me, "What do you say, Blue?"

I nodded.

"Sounds good," said Pete, looking back at Mack.

Just then, the train give a whistle and we heard the brakes vent steam.

"Last call," Pete said. "It's leaving."

"I'm in," I said. And we watched until the train pulled off and we saw the caboose lights disappear.

"Got a match?" Mack asked.

Pete took his matches from the satchel and the two men made a small fire where Mack had absentmindedly already started piling kindling while we talked. I helped by adding some wood scraps I found nearby, until the pain in my palm reminded me I had struck the cinders when Pete pushed me from the train. The pain shot through my wrist when I picked up the first piece of wood and I realized my palm was sticky. Pete saw me wince.

"Better come over here to the light, Blue."

I held my hand out to the firelight. The warmth felt good on my cold fingers.

"Yeah," said Pete, taking my wrist and turning it toward the light. "You got some cinders imbedded under the skin. Light's not good enough to clean it tonight. Better wash your wound and put it up in a bandage for the night."

Pete took a small canteen out of his satchel and poured a bit of water from it onto my hand. Stung a bit. Then he stripped the bandana from around his neck and wrapped it around my hand.

"That should keep it from bleeding anymore and from getting infected until we can check it in daylight. Now, go finish getting the wood and we'll get you warm."

I finished gathering the wood and before long we was warming off the chill June evening air.

Mack fumbled in a pocket and took out a half-smoked cig.

He held the stump between the gap in his teeth and leaned forward to light it from a stick he took from the fire. The end glowed red and for the first time, I saw Mack's bloodshot eyes. I turned away so he wouldn't think I was staring.

"Smoke?" asked Mack, handing the butt off to me.

Mama would skin me alive if she ever saw me touch one. Pete took it instead and dragged one puff before handing it back to Mack.

"Thanks," said Pete.

"Hey, won't somebody see our fire and hassle us?" I asked.

"Jesus Christ, kid, you are a virgin," Mack said. "First no smoke and then worrying about the fire."

"Leave the kid alone," said Pete. "We better get some sleep."

"Hey, I didn't mean nothing by it, fella," argued Mack, but Pete just ignored him and I could see by the look on his face, Mack wasn't used to being ignored.

My stomach grumbled from not having eaten since morning.

"I got some eggs," I said. I figured eating without sharing with Pete and Mack would have been nigh to impossible and probably not polite.

Mack grabbed one eagerly and began peeling the shell, but Pete said "No thanks, Kid, you better eat it."

Pete placed his cap on the ground, smoothed it out like he was smoothing out a pillow, and laid down facing the tracks. I did the same with my backside to the fire because my rump was cold from sitting on the ground and I ate my egg in silence. Lying there, already farther from home than I ever been, I wondered if my folks missed me. It was the first night, I told myself, and I promised myself to keep count.

June 19, 1937

Next Town

I would discover along the way that "Next Town" was a pretty big place. It seemed to stretch clear across the country. Every hobo had been to Next Town. None was ever welcome to stay.

Sunny and warm as the next day turned out to be, morning was nothing but wet—a kind of dampness that makes your clothes stick to your skin and keeps you chilled until almost noon.

Thanks to Pete, my hand wasn't swollen but it was sure enough sore. By the light of day, Pete unwrapped the makeshift bandage and was able to see the cinders imbedded in my hand. He cleaned me up proper while Mack stoked up a fire and put a pot of chicory to brewing.

Never really had chicory before but I heard my pa mention it from his boyhood days. It weren't as strong as real coffee and a lot more bitter than Mama's coffee, and we had no sugar to sweeten it neither. But it was a good wake up for a man, as Mack said. Back home, Mama said drinking coffee was no good for a growing boy as it would stunt his growth. All she ever give me was coffee-milk, a cup of milk when we could get it and a spoonful or two of coffee for taste. I reckon I done most of my growing now so I took a cup when it was ready. I guess I don't see the fascination with the stuff but on that damp morning the mug sure felt good between my hands, once I was bandaged up again of course.

Well, Pete took out his penknife and held it over the fire a little.

"Wish we had a little whiskey," he said, looking over at Mack hopefully.

I was thinking I didn't really want to drink no whiskey but then he said "to pour over the knife and wound."

Mack shrugged, but I saw the look in his red eyes. They weren't so red this morning, but I figured he was holding out.

"This will have to do then," said Pete, then he commenced to digging at the biggest piece of cinder.

It couldn'ta been much larger than a pea but it hurt like the dickens. He squeezed the flesh and it hurt even worse. I cussed, then blushed and told my mama I was sorry, though she weren't there to hear me. Pa woulda winked from knowing sometimes a cuss word just come out when a man didn't know what else to say. Mama said cussing was a sign of an uneducated man. I didn't know who was right because about then, I was watching the blood rise on my palm.

"Whatcha want to go and do that for?" I asked Pete.

"The bleeding will help wash out any dirt that might cause an infection later," he said. "The other two or three pieces are too small to dig out. We'll just have to keep your hand as clean as possible and keep the bandage on. I'll check it later."

Pete stuffed his knife back in his pocket and I got to thinkin' on Billy Sawyer's pa. He worked in the coal mines and had black spots permanently ground into his face and hands. I reckoned those small black spots of cinder in my hand, that looked like dirt, would never disappear, no matter how much these hands of mine get washed.

With my hand all bandaged and our coffee drunk, we reckoned we better light out for Next Town if we wanted to reach it by dark. Mack had business there, and although I was eager to see

Mrs. Roosevelt, Pete and I decided to tag along on foot next day. We followed the tracks as long as there weren't no trains come by.

The landscape was different than where we lived in the hills. Here it was more like rolling hills than the steeper ones back home. Fewer trees too but that was the railroad's doing. They cut down a lot of the trees to make ties and to keep the trains safe. They burned off the brush but you can't keep the wild out. It grows back almost as fast as they can cut and burn. So the tracks was lined here and there with scrub brush. Some of the scrub was berries, and the edible kind too. If it weren't for me, the fellas wouldn't know'd what kind to pick. They musta been city-folk. Our travel was uneventful but we had a capful of berries, what Mama called "lusciousness," to pick on at lunchtime and later for supper, though neither was filling. You learn to be mighty grateful for anything that ain't dirt when you can get a meal.

As the day wore on with the sun more direct overhead, it got mighty hot even for June. I took off Pete's borrowed shirt and pulled the top of my overalls down, tucking the shirt into the band of my underwear. My back sure got sweated up and the dust along the tracks just caked to it by the time we hit an open field and Next Town come into view. It was just before sunset and by then I was carrying my shoes, walking barefoot. We seen the town lights just beginning to turn on in the shadowed places, could even smell the wood-smoke in the air. Finally, we come to a Hooverville situated just outside town limits.

I ain't never seen one until then but the fellas at the barbershop talked about them—so many folks out of work and out of their homes. What did they say now? Foreclosed, that was it. Foreclosed. Had the banks take their homes clean away and most without time to even pack their things. Well all those folks without homes seemed to gravitate to towns, probably looking for work and charity. Without much of either to be given, they just settled right where they was at the time, in whatever tents and makeshift structures they could muster up. The authorities would try to run them off but even they didn't have the heart as long as squatters was obeying the law and the land owner didn't mind. Only now, as we got closer I could see it weren't so much a Hooverville as it was a Jungle, a hobo town, and I didn't much care for the look of the fellas there neither.

Musta been about twenty or so shacks made of cardboard, scrap wood, scrub brush, and whatever they could find to build. Men and boys like me was gathered all round in clusters. Some had small fires going for their grub. Some talked in pairs and small groups. The smoke clung to the ground in the heavy night air. The campfires madea reddish glow on the fellas' faces. Some mangy old dogs scrapped over what could be found. Heard a loud yelp as a man kicked out at a dog trying to snatch at a hunk of fat he'd slung over a make-shift spit.

As we approached, one by one, like in slow motion, men stood and turned to watch us. A wisp of dust rose up from the trampled ground of the camp as we walked. I ain't never seen such hollowed out looks in men's faces—dirty, covered in worry, like they was already dead and buried. And ragged? Lord, they was a ragged bunch and only the first of many I would see.

Mack, without any explanation, just walked on up to one of the men and started talking. He was pointing back at us and it give me a chill. I reckon the man he was talking to was some kind of boss man, though I doubted men on the road would pay much attention to one if they didn't have a liking to what he had to say.

I seen the man nod in our direction and Mack motioned for us to come on over. Two other men squatting nearby stood up slow-like. They was threatening. One had a stick he kept on slapping in his hand while glaring at Pete and me. He spat on the ground and the other man give his head a nudge for us to keep going. Don't know why I figured hobos would be more welcoming of their own kind but when we finally sat by Lou's fire, the man Mack was talking to. Lou said they was being extra cautious about detectives and besides there weren't no work in town more than they was already doing and he warned us outright to move on come morning.

Lou said, "These boys don't really have to listen to me when I tell 'em you ain't figuring to stake claim to their jobs. So you better just sleep with one eye open and be off at first light if you know what's good for ya."

I don't mind saying, it was all right with me. And as far as I was concerned, I didn't intend to fall asleep at all.

I had a little time to walk around before sunset, just to get a better idea of what Pete and me got ourselves into, I guess. I wanted to be sure I know where everybody was housed and how to find the way out in the middle of the night if we needed to light. I swear, them shacks was hardly big enough for one man to sleep full out and some I expect had to curl in a ball to fit out of the rain when it come, and even then I doubted most of the roofs would even keep out the rain. There wouldn't be no cover for us, Lou said. We'd have to sleep in the open but we was welcome near the fire if we wanted. Not sure exactly why but Mack seemed right at home there and right comfortable to take a shack for his bed, though he swore he didn't live there, he only passed through now and then.

Pete and me made ourselves as comfortable as we could by the fire. I was getting mighty hungry about that time and thinking about Mama. We didn't have much, to be sure, but her cooking almost felt like a feast in my memory right about then.

"Pete, you reckon any of these fellas might have some food to spare?"

I knew it was a foolish question as soon as I asked it. Those men hardly had enough to feed themselves, let alone to spare. But I was surprised when Mack walked over and tossed a can of beans to Pete.

"Can't see my fellow travelers go hungry, now can I?"

"Much obliged," said Pete. Then to me he added. "Nothing in this world is ever free, remember that Blue."

All I know is hot on the fire or cold out of the can, those beans was gonna be like a full course meal.

As we was feasting, we talked some.

"Sure was some day," I said.

"Yep," Pete replied with a mouth full. "I am grateful it was an uneventful day." Beginning to unlace his shoes, he seemed to think better of it and tied them back up again. "Better sleep with your shoes on tonight, Blue." He winked and put a hand on my shoulder. "Just to be sure. Will you do that?"

"Yeah, I reckon," I said. "How far from Wellsboro do you think we come?"

I could almost see the wheels turning in Pete's head as he did some arithmetic.

"Well, we rode the train yesterday and it probably took us a full fifty mile, maybe seventy-five. We walked a slow meandering bit today, so maybe another fifteen. I think I heard one of the men say the little town yonder is Selinsburg or Selinsgrove. Something like that."

"You plan to go into town in the morning?"

"Blue, I plan to do just like Lou said . . . leave before daybreak. You're welcome to keep with me."

Good lord, I surely planned to do that. It was somewhat comforting to hear the invite, though I do admit, town sounded tempting. Pa called wishing "Self-fulfillin' prophecy." Mama scolded him saying weren't no such thing as prophecy lessin' the Good Lord brung it and it was downright hedonistic to think on such things. Then Pa would explain what he meant.

"If a man, or a woman," he added looking at Mama, "should imagine hisself as lazy good for nothin', then he will be lazy and good for nothin'. But if a man, or a woman, thinks hisself a child of God and God being

righteous and all, then that man is likened to God and will live Godly and well."

Whenever Pa put God in anything he said, Mama was less likely to argue the point and he knew it. Sometimes I had to translate his words in my own head to really understand it. He was saying, if I thought myself well-to-do, I'd become well to do, or at least I'd never be a poor man. If I believed myself intelligent and strong, well, I'd be just that. I seen plenty of boys in school teased by other fellas into believing themselves to be less than nothing and indeed they didn't amount to much.

Mama always said there's a power to words, and she was right.

Unfortunately, I made a wish that night to go to town in the morning but I forgot to wish Pete into it.

***

Now when the men told us that night to skedaddle before daybreak, Pete didn't take it on the chin. Instead he said back to them, he'd put some thought on their advice, but we was sorely in need of supplies. He said it would behoove us to make a quick stop in town before heading out.

Must be those fellas didn't like his answer because it was sometime, maybe an hour or so after I fell asleep mind you, I'm guessing on the time, but I was wide awake enough to know what was happening.

First, I heard low voices and I seen our fire was just a few embers by then. I thought it might queer to hear somebody whispering nearby, but I just turned my backside to the fire. When I still felt the night chill and recalled not putting Pete's shirt back on, I decided to do so right then. I turned back over to get it from where I set it beside Pete's pack and then I seen them. Two of the roughs we had seen earlier, one had been holding the stick, they was rifling through Pete's satchel!

Took but a second for my eyes to adjust to the half dark, then I seen another man. It was Mack! He was sitting on Pete and give him a smack in the jaw.

"Hey, you!" I shouted, scrambling to my feet. "Let go!" I was shouting about both Pete and his bag but they didn't pay no mind.

"Lou!" Mack yelled. "Get that blasted kid out of here."

Lou leaped across the campfire and tagged me before I could run. We scuffled a bit. He tried putting his hand over my mouth but I bit him good.

"Yeow! The brat gnawed on me!"

The other man was laughing. I don't know why nobody woke up with his yelp but if they did, they didn't come running. Mack pulled Pete to his feet. With his weight, and coming on Pete in his sleep, Mack had an unfair advantage. Pete tried to return the blow, but I seen him stagger. One more punch from Mack and Pete went down. I lowered my head and threw myself at Lou's midriff aiming to knock the wind out of him.

"You can't hit him like that, you no good . . . "

My complaint was silenced when Lou's knee come up in my chin. It knocked some mighty sense into me and I fell back, but as I fell I grabbed his foot and pushed him backwards. Lou landed in the fire. I was flat on my back but raised my head and seen him rolling to one side and his friend beating a flame out of his sleeve.

"Why, you!" Lou had murder in his eyes as he turned on me again.

All I could see as he leaped on me was Mack pulling Pete to his feet then letting him fall in a limp pile. It was the last I seen. Lou's fist caught my jaw and everything went black. That was my second night.

A Bad Seed

When I woke, I was on a pile of rags serving for a bed in one of the shacks, or least that's what I thought. Mack was sitting not far away since the quarters was so close. My head was on fire. I tried sitting up.

"Pete?"

"Yer uncle ain't here, boy."

"He ain't . . ."

I was about to say, *"Ain't my uncle,"* but now I knew what he meant by big rock candy mountain. He thought I was Pete's "boy." About then I had a picture in my head—a foggy picture like a rain-covered window in the back of my mind. In it, I seen Pete fall and Mack standing over him. Pete weren't moving.

I sat up with a start but the pain shot through my head. I thought I might vomit, the room did a spin, and I slumped back with a groan. All I could muster before going black was, "You no good dirty . . . " I wanted to ask what he did with Pete but nothing worked right then. The room spun "Veni vidi . . . " Blackness.

***

I reckon somebody musta give me water—maybe broth—I can't be sure, but I was told I was out for days and musta hit my head on a rock when Lou walloped me. I did have a mighty painful lump on the back of my head and a cracked lip already swollen and turned black. It wasn't until after I returned home and Mama had the doc look me over, that he said I was lucky I didn't die with a cracked skull.

Once I woke again, Mack come over and said he figured I must be hungry, which I sure enough was.

"Just so happens," he said, "one of the other boys got some bread from town." Mack had bargained enough to spare for me.

I was too hungry to ask where Pete was, which is what I wanted to know most. Instead I said, "Much obliged," and proceeded tearing the bread apart and shoveling it in, forgetting any manners Mama had taught me. I was just an animal with needs. She'd hardly recognize me with a swollen face covered with dried blood and three days or more of dirt.

"Gotta get some water," I said.

I went to rise up but Mack said, "You been down without any real substance for a while now. You better take it easy at first."

Mack handed me an old bean can filled with water. After I drunk it, he held out his hand to help me to my feet. I just wanted to be out in the light of day, which I sensed from the sun oozing through the cracks in the shanty's boarded walls. Mack decided it would be good to walk me around outside a bit.

A few men and boys milled about in front of various shacks. They stared at us, and I seen some of the men put their hands on the boys' shoulders. The boys didn't look too keen on it, but they didn't pull away or nothing.

"Some of the men have lit out," Mack said. "They come and go. And some is in town looking for work or food."

I expected the boy who brung me some bread was there in camp but Mack didn't say. I would have liked to thank him but I never found out who he was and as it turned out, it didn't matter. The boys did whatever they was told to do, as I would soon learn. For now, I walked with Mack's help and then I got some more sleep.

***

Like I said, Mack give me water. A man can't go without it for long. He can live a month without food but not water, only living without food was no small task. I was almost starving come next morning.

I felt a whole lot better except for the knot of hunger in my stomach and the stiff lip. Mack was not in the shack so I got up and looked around for my shoes. Nope. They was no place to be seen, but Pete's shirt was there and I put it on. *Pete. What did they do with Pete?*

Outside, I found the usual gang of unkempt boys and men, and Mack. He motioned for me to join him by the fire. It was a fair enough June morning—leastwise I thought it was still June, and I reckoned by the sun it was nearing noon.

"Coffee?" Mack asked. He had already started to pour. He handed me a cup and I sat on a log nearby. "You must be a heap of hungry."

"I sure could eat something," I said. I didn't trust Mack. How could I? "You know, I been thinking about Pete." I waited, measuring his response. He didn't even look away from his cup. "That night you hit him, I been wondering why, and where he is."

"Boy," Mack hissed, then he changed his tone—added some sugar to it as Mama would say. "Your friend cleared out at morning's light like he was asked and he told me to look after you."

It seemed a reasonable thing. Pete did seem like the kind of fella who would think rest was better for me than tagging along with him on the road.

"But what about the fight?" I asked.

"That, son, was a private beef and I reckon you should ask Pete if you ever catch up with him."

Suddenly things went strange. Mack come over and sat next to me.

"You know son," he said putting a hand on my knee, "you can stay here. I got a feeling you'd fit right in."

Now my pa and me had loads of what he called "chats about life." Pa put his hand on my knee and give it a tap many a time, but I never had a growed man, I didn't know, squeeze my knee the way Mack did. It made me uneasy, to say the least. If I was hungry, I reckon I lost my appetite, even after he changed his tone and got all business-like.

"In fact, I got some work for you."

"Well now, I wouldn't mind doing no work and it's right neighborly of you, but I reckon as soon as I get something to eat, I'll hit the road looking for P . . . looking for Pa." The glare Mack give me at the sound of "P" made me stop what I was going to say and change directions. "Pa left home on Mama and I am looking to bring him back. That's what I intend to do."

I felt the fires of hell burning the soles of my feet like Mama said they would if I lied, but this was a necessity and Pa said, "*Sometimes necessity will cause a man to do what he knows is wrong to save his life and God will forgive him.*"

"I see," said Mack. "Well, you can go looking for your Pa but you ain't eating unless you do some work for it. I know you're hungry but every man and boy here pulls his weight or he don't eat, and that's a fact."

Mack's voice had raised a might and now the others, scattered about camp, all seemed to be looking at us.

"All right then, I'll work for my food and then I'm gone."

"Good," said Mack, putting his hand on my shoulder this time and then moving his arm so it was around my shoulder like I seen some of the other men with their arms around the boys. It made my skin crawl. Then Mack added, "Long as we have an understanding. Now, finish your coffee. You have a job to do."

I wasn't much for the coffee right then. I took another sip but tossed the rest away and threw Mack's cup on the ground by the fire. He had started walking toward his shanty and I followed him inside.

Mack had Pete's satchel in hand and tossed it at me. I caught it and the leather made a soft thud it makes when it hits a solid, albeit hungry body.

"You're going to town."

"Hey," I complained, "this is Pete's satchel." I glared at Mack and felt white heat rise up behind my ears. "You take this from him?"

"Boy, I got it, don't I? Your friend . . . "

"His name is Pete!"

"Very well then. Pete left it when he lit out and said you was to have it."

"What about . . . " I paused, thinking if I dared to ask about Pete's watch. But then, if he had left on his own, he would have taken it with him for sure. What if he hadn't left on his own? What if they dumped him or worse, killed him? A little voice told me I should keep quiet. Pa always said a man needs to pick his fights and know when to shut up.

"What about what?"

"Uh, my shoes. What about my shoes?"

"Well now, shoes is hard to come by and Lord knows what happened to them. You can't leave things laying about, boy—they's liable to go missing."

I was boiling mad—angry to my very core. First Pete, and now my shoes! My only good-for-Sunday shoes!

"I can't and I won't go to town without shoes!"Mack took a step toward me with his hand raised. I cringed; still feeling the last time a grown man hit me in the face. He seen me and withdrew his hand.

"Good," he said. "Remember your place here and you'll be all right. Now, here is what's gonna happen . . ."

The Job

I promised myself to keep track of the days. I failed to keep my promise. I had no idea how long I'd been unconscious. Maybe five days? So I'd been on the road at least one week.

In such a short time, I'd been chased by bulls, had cinders permanently imbedded in my hand, the life beaten out of me, my shoes stolen, and possibly been a witness to murder. I was thinking of Pete. Now, I was in a tight spot, being a kept-boy with some bum, and about to become a criminal by robbing the Selinsgrove First National Bank.

Mack's orders was clear. "Walk into town, stay out of sight as much as possible and don't talk to no one. Go straight to the bank, tell the man in the cage to fill the satchel, and point this here pistol at his face. If he don't do what you say, shoot it once at the ceiling and next time at his head."

It was a horrific thought. I never killed, never entertained such thoughts. I could never ever kill nobody, no how. But if I didn't do as Mack said, I wouldn't eat and I'm telling you I was powerful hungry enough. When I said I'd go, my shoes was found right quick. To be sure I did as I was told, Lou was to walk with me as far as the first buildings in town then split off to where he could keep watch on me from a distance.

So this was why they got rid of Pete and kept me behind. This was the work Mack had in town. Nothing legitimate. He musta been there before and couldn't dare show his face. He said there was a payroll coming in and if he pulled off this heist, he wouldn't be riding rails no more. And what of me? Well, I suppose he didn't care. If I got found out and throwed in jail, he'd be off safe someplace. And if I told on him, they wouldn't find him. I'd go down the river and he'd be scot-free. Or what if I got killed? Well, it would be no skin off Mack's nose, but Mama wouldn't be none too happy either way. No sir, I was just not gonna do this. I was determined. Yet there was Lou always breathing down my neck.

***

"Okay kid, here's where we part ways. Just you remember, I'm watchin' you. You do any funny business and you're on your own. I catch ya, and you'll rue the day."

Lou handed the pistol toward me. My hand shook so much, I had to grab it with both, using one to keep the other steady. I felt the weight of that cold steel and couldn't even bring myself to look at it as I stuffed it in my pocket. Lord help me.

"You hear me kid?"

"Yeah, I hear ya."

I could tell Lou didn't much like the look I give him.

"Don't be a wise guy. Mind you, do as you was told, or else."

He put two fingers to his eyes and pointed them at me.

"I'm watching you."

The gun was heavy in my pocket. I just took Mack's word that it was loaded and prayed I wouldn't need it. In fact, I prayed I might just as well drop dead before I entered the building because there was no way this plan was going to work. No way I was going through with it. Then I almost doubled over with hunger pangs. Was it really so bad taking money from a bank that had loads of dough to spare? I sure was hungry.

I turned the corner and almost ran headfirst into a man carrying a valise.

"Careful there, son," he said.

He scared me so much, I nearly jumped out of my skin.

Mack had loaned me a cap and I pulled it down over my eyes in an attempt to hide my swollen jaw in the shadow of the brim. I watched from the corner of my eye as the man crossed the street. I turned back to look for Lou. He was nowhere to be seen but no doubt he could see me.

The main street in Selinsgrove was called Market Street and it was probably just about like any other small-town, USA, but I could tell it had some history. The street was lined with brick buildings with small white turned-rail porches, some with a flower box or two. I reckoned from my schoolbooks it looked like some of it was here around the Civil War and maybe even earlier. I later found out it was settled by a general from the Revolutionary War, but right then I didn't have no time to think on it. I was looking for the bank, though I'd rather not.

Old street lamps—probably gas at one time—stood like black-painted iron sentinels all up one side and down the other. There was a narrow strip of green down the center of town with a gazebo in the middle. I looked up both sides of town. I come out from Walnut Street and south of me was a church. North was the main downtown shopping district. An occasional automobile moved slowly down the paved street. A wood-sided panel truck turned the corner. A few cars sat parked along the curbs—it was a small-ish town after all. I seen a store with barrels in the front and the walkway ran underneath the roof overhang. It had to be the general store. Next to that was the barber pole.

I seen some men carrying music cases climbing the gazebo steps, and ten or twenty town folk begun gathering on the green to sit on the benches around the bandstand. Mack told me the town had music every Tuesday at noon, and sure enough he was right. He said the music would draw the crowds away from the bank, and the bank teller would be closing up his cage for lunch in the park. Mack had cased it all out. I couldn't tarry none too long. I stepped up my pace.

I walked past the general store and behind a delivery truck parked in front, then past the barbershop. I took a quick glance in the barbershop window. Looked like the one back home only neater.

Inside the barbershop I seen only the barber and a customer in the chair with his face all lathered up. I reckon the old men who usually hung around such places were over in the park. What I wouldn't have given to walk in and sit myself down to hide from Lou, but his eyes just kept burning a hole in the back of my head. I knew he had me eyed.

Beyond the park, on the other side of the road like a mirror image of the old general store, was a newer Five & Dime. Surely wanted to take a look—never been in one of them. But time was ticking and the church steeple bell begun to ring the noon hour just as the band was tuning up for their first piece.

Just about half a city block away was the Selinsgrove First National Bank. I caught some movement out of the corner of my eye and seen a police car pull up to the police station, which was across Market on the other side of the green. My heart jumped. The bank door was in view of the police station, which brung me back to my situation. Bank, police, gun, music drifting across the street. My heart was pounding out a beat in my ears. I suddenly felt sick. Two more steps and I would be at the bank door. Once inside, there would be no turning back. I felt my stomach tie in a knot.

For the first time since Lou handed me the gun, I couldn't force the truth out of my mind with my daydreamin'. There was one reason I was here. I come to rob a bank to pay for a meal and if not, the only thing waiting worse than the hunger was a severe beating. Then I seen it—the sign in the bank window just being turned over by the banker. "Closed for Lunch."

I missed it! No, it couldn't be! I took hold of the door handle. Locked! I tugged and rattled it in hopes it was just stuck and the banker hadn't locked it yet, but it didn't budge. Shading my eyes with my right hand, I put my face up to the door. Squinting, I just caught a glimpse of the banker disappearing into what I assumed was his office. *Should I knock? Would he hear me? And if he come to the door, would he even let me in looking ragged as I did?* I doubted it. *Now what?*

The whole plan had been to slip in quiet-like as the band begun to play, and to walk without hesitation to the teller's cage and demand the cash. *Now what was I gonna do?* I reckoned I could wait for the banker, but then maybe the band-concert would be over. I failed. Then I remembered Lou. If he was indeed watching me, he was seeing this whole scene. I looked over my shoulder and seen his checkered shirt, tan trousers, and beat-up fedora as he moved across the green toward me in a fast walk. Reckon that was what they meant on the radio shows when they said "The jig is up. I tasted bile and spat as I surveyed my surroundings for a place to run. And I did run, like I was being chased by the devil, only this devil was Lou.

I always had this unusual idea that if you can't see them, they can't see you. Sounds strange, no doubt, but it works like this. Say you're hiding in the woods. You are behind a big ole tree and your cousin is trying to find you. Well, if you is hid enough and peek 'round but can't see them, then probably they can't see you neither. I wasn't changing my way of thinking with Lou. I wasn't looking for him and I hope my idea was working and he wasn't seeing me.

I didn't look back. I just run the opposite direction of the green, down East Pine, dodged an automobile, and continued until I seen a picket fence. I could usually hop a fence like that one, but I had no strength and barely cleared it. My overalls caught on the peak of the fence post. I turned head over heels into someone's yard. They had laundry hanging on the line and it made a perfect shield to duck under. I waited a tick, caught my breath, then scrambled to my feet. Then I come face to face with the lady of the house carrying another basket of clothes to the line. She was about to scream.

Breathing heavy I blurted, "Please, Ma'am, don't yell. There's a real bad man following me."

Without thinking, I reached in my pocket, took out the pistol, shoved it in her hand, and kept on running before she had time to realize what just happened. I jumped the fencerow behind the houses and come out in an alley on the other side. No sign of Lou.

Guess I sat there in the alley behind a pile of crates for hours and musta finally give Lou the slip. He didn't show. I also guess I fell asleep because when I woke the sun was starting to set. Since I been on the road at least a week, it was almost summer. I figured it was about eight or maybe closer to nine o'clock. Then I heard one of Mama's old favorite hymns.

Shall we gather at the river
where bright angel feet have trod,
with its crystal tide forever
flowing by the throne of God?
Yes, we'll gather at the river,
the beautiful, the beautiful river;
gather with the saints at the river
that flows by the throne of God.

Surely seemed like a fitting song for the end of day as I looked out over the Susquehanna River flowing by Selinsgrove. I made a plan to visit the river next morning for a much needed bath. Right then, however, more than any bath, I needed a meal, and I knew what the singing meant. It meant the Salvation Army— hot coffee, and maybe a hot supper and a bed, even if I had to sit through the sermon first.

I dusted myself off by slapping my cap on my sleeves and pant legs. Woulda licked down my hair but my hands was so grubby, even I wouldn't shake one, let alone put my tongue to it. I crept slowly to the end of the alley and looked up the street to be sure the coast was clear, then rounded the corner onto Snyder Street. Looking eastward to the end of the street, I could still see the big ole river through the trees. If my book learning served me, the Susquehanna run from the foothills of New York State all the way to the Chesapeake Bay and was the longest river on this side of the country. This was mighty pretty country too. Lush and green. If the river didn't snake so much, I surely would have followed it almost to Washington.

In the twilight haze, the street lamps begun a soft glow, and a warm light gleamed through an old storefront at the end of the block. The sign overhead said *Salvation Army*. A lady in white gloves, wearing a crisp navy blue uniform with a matching hat stood at the door.

"God bless you, son," she said with a pleasant smile. *Finally somebody smiling who didn't mean they was really frowning on the inside.* "Come in out of the damp." She handed me a leaflet. There was a picture of some homeless folk and I just made out the words, "Let us feed your stomach and your soul. Salvation Army."

I thanked her, and like Mama taught me I removed my cap as I stepped across the threshold. The air was comfortable, not too hot inside. There was a small front room with the shop windows facing the street, rows of chairs facing a podium at the front of the room. There was a table set up to the left with coffee, cream, sugar, and some cups. Cookies, too. At the front of the room was two men, one with a coronet and the other with a tuba. They wasn't playing just then. Three ladies and a man was leading the congregated in the hymn I heard. I sung along and thought of Mama as I made my way to a seat.

There was about ten men and two other boys standing at the seats, and I joined them. When the hymn was finished, one of the Brothers said, "Amen," and we all sat down. Felt mighty good to sit even on a hard wooden chair.

"Brothers," said the same Soldier of God. "Let us pray. Oh God, thank you for bringing these your children to us tonight. Hold them in the warmth of your love, give them sustenance, and help them find their way. Amen."

"Amen."

"Now, if y'all want to get yourself some coffee and a cookie or two, and join us back at your seats, we have a few words to say before taking you to dine and finding you a bed for the night."

I was thinking *I surely wish you'd just show us to the table.* But I knew it wouldn't be polite.

The woman handing out the coffee was probably the first aside from my mama to take note of my eyes. She just didn't take her eyes off them.

"You have the bluest eyes I've ever seen," she said.

I replied, "Only next to my pa."

"What is your name, son?"

"Blue, Ma'am. Just Blue."

"Well, Blue, welcome and I hope your stay is comfortable."

She was really right pretty and I expect she mighta been a heap prettier if she showed her hair instead of having it in a bun. I think I blushed.

The coffee was strong. But the cookie, well it could been a cow pie and I wouldn'ta noticed, because I was so hungry. The boy sitting next to me seen how I gobbled it down and I reckon he didn't like his much because he silently handed it sideways to me. I hesitated.

"Take it," he said, only he weren't a 'he.' Couldn't tell until he spoke but he was a 'she.' "Don't tell," she whispered. "They don't allow girls here."

Brother John give a right decent sermon, standing there at the podium flanked by the American and the Salvation Army flags, though I mighta been the only one really paying attention. Then the Sisters and Brothers told us the rules and regulations.

"No drinking. No smoking. No cussing. And, no stealing. Men get two meals and two nights stay. Boys get two meals and one night stay, no exceptions. Boys are expected to clear out after breakfast and head on home."

The rules was pretty austere and forthright. They didn't say nothing about girls, so my new pal was safe. Her name, as it turned out, was Penny, though she said to call her Pete, for now. Now, weren't it an interesting circumstance? And once we left the Salvation Army, I seen why her name was Penny. In the sunlight, that girl's hair was the shiniest copper color I ever seen, though she had chopped it down like a boy.

June 30, 1937

A Penny for Your Thoughts

They had a calendar at the Salvation Army and I seen the date.

Ten days! I wasn't making much progress toward my goal of meeting Mrs. Roosevelt, and it looked like I would have to spin my wheels for a few more. I needed some supplies, food, money, and I still wanted to find out if anyone had seen Pete. It just didn't sit right with me to think of leaving after he had helped me, without at least asking around a while. I knew Mrs. Roosevelt wasn't going nowhere, but then there was Pa. He *was* mighty sick. Still I needed those supplies, and it meant looking for bona fide work and keeping my distance from the jungle. Lou and Mack musta been sorely angry and fit to be tied.

***

Morning was hot and clear, and it proved a fine day to get in a swim but I really didn't need it after my night at the Salvation Army, the way they made us clean up. The night before, they give us a bowl with a bar of Ivory Soap for washing and a toothbrush with baking soda and salt. I felt almost human again. Nothing feels so good as running your tongue over squeaky-clean teeth, I must say.

I cupped my hand over my mouth and blowed, then breathed it in quick. My breath smelled so much better.

First, we ate a breakfast of coffee, toast, oatmeal, and a small slice of ham. I thought I'd died and gone to heaven on that meal. And talk about comfort. The cots weren't too bad, and we each had a hand-sewn quilt made by the ladies auxiliary, with a feather pillow! Imagine, a real pillow. You sure can miss the simple things when you're far from home.

After breakfast, and morning-prayer, the lady with the nice smile, Sister Sarah, said goodbye and pointed us to the police station where she fully expected us kids to report ourselves and go on home. Penny and the other boy from that night—his name was Fred—and me promised Sister Sarah to do as she said, only we crossed our fingers behind our back so as not to lie. I thought it was pleasant of them not to turn us over to the police. I reckon they didn't want to get too involved, as they had seen arrests go bad. Us three just marched on west, down Snyder Street in the direction she pointed, then doubled back through the same alley I'd been to the night before, then on over to the river.

The river it turned out, was split down the middle by Penns Creek—a small tributary—and an island. Now, we got the full scope and size of that mighty river. Took my breath away.

"What you reckon you'll do now?" Fred asked Penny.

She took off her cap and I give a whistle after seeing her hair, and shielded my eyes with my hand like I was looking into the sun.

Penny glared and slapped me on the head with the cap. "Think I ain't heard that joke before, Breadline?"

Fred give out a roaring laugh, "Breadline! Good one, Penny." Fred pointed at me. "Breadline Blue is your name for sure!"

We all laughed and pulled off our shoes. Penny ran down the bank to the creek's edge, pulled off her jacket, and proceeded to strip down to her shorts and undershirt. I naturally looked away.

Fred took off behind her, and looking back at me shouted, "Ain't you never seen a girl's underthings afore? 'Sides, they's boys' anyway! Come on, Breadline, the water's fine!"

By then, Penny had dove in and Fred was on her tail. This was a strange adventure, I thought, and getting stranger all the time. Swimming with girls in their brother's underwear. Lordy.

Fred was sure enough right about the water. Throwing my shoes on the ground with my cap and shirt, I stripped myself down to my drawers too and dove. It felt so like heaven, the clean cold water on a late June morning in the sun. It just rushed over my head and along my limbs and I was baptized all over again. The dirt and sweat and stink the Ivory Soap didn't find just fairly swirled around me and washed away.

I come up to the surface. "Yee Haw!"

After a good night's sleep on a full belly, and now some enjoyment with folks close to my own age, I felt like brand new.

There was some mighty big trees along that part of the island and one had a rope hanging off a long limb reaching over the bank to the water. I never seen someone do so well at rope swinging as Penny and she could swim just fine too, for a girl.

We splashed around, come out, and dove in again, dunking each other and playing water tag. Then, the three of us threw ourselfs full-out on the grassy bank to sun-dry like three lizards on a rock. Lord have mercy, I can't recall the last time I had such a smileful morning.

"You never said, Penny," I spoke while pulling a piece of sweet grass to chew on.

"Said what?"

"Fred asked what you was planning to do next. You never said."

"Well now, I'm heading south to Richmond. I got an Aunt Milly there I'm fixin' to call on."

"Why'd you run off in the first place?" Fred asked. "I run off cuz my pa boxed my ears good one day for smokin' a corn silk then commenced to tellin' me how I was too old to take care of no more and I should just get out. It was just about the same time he took another slug on the corn liquor. I reckon I didn't want to get beat no more. But why'd you leave? Somebody beatin' on you, too?"

"Hell's bells," Penny laughed, sitting up and shaking the wet out of her cropped hair. "I left to see the sights."

"Won't your ma miss you?" I asked.

"Look here, Blue, I got five brothers and two younger sisters. I helped raise them all after my pa lit out. I watched my ma practically work herself to death. Then, one day after my oldest brother—who is just seventeen mind you, I'm thirteen—after he told Ma he got his girl Becky with child, I decided right then I wasn't wasting my life away in that town no more."

Penny dove back in the creek and swam to the mainland shore, climbed out, and begun getting her clothes on, which signaled us that the day's games was over. We followed, and she finished what she was saying.

"I got an aunt in Richmond supposed to have a house and some cash. I reckon to visit her and if she likes me well enough, ask if I can stay. She never married and got none of her own." Penny tied her shoe. "And what about you, Breadline? What you got goin'?"

I was reluctant to say. I mean, I figured it might sound pretty lame to them with all they been through, telling them I was going to Washington to see the president's wife and ask for her help. Truth be told, right then, it sounded lame to me, too.

"Aw, I got good folks. My pa ain't well and Mama's busy caring for him. I'm just looking to make my way and maybe help out once I figure it out for myself."

We was all dressed again and Penny had already begun walking back toward town. Fred slapped my back. "You can find odd-jobs in town if you look," he said. "Let's go see what can we find."

***

Back in town, we walked down Snyder, past the Salvation Army, trying not to be seen. Penny run past, with Fred on her heels, and me laughing so hard I almost peed myself. We cut over Second to Pine, then on up Water Street to avoid the police at Market and Pine. Finally, we come to street that gave me a kick—Sassafras Street! How it got its name, I don't know, but there was a couple small factories. For all I knew, maybe they made sassafras on that street.

"You ever drunk sassafras, Penny? Fred?"

"Nope," she said, "but my ma makes sassafras soap and I knew a lady once who used it for perfume. Smells kinda nice, ya know?"

"I drunk it," said Fred. "You do know that's what they use to make root beer?"

"Really?" Penny said, with a hint of sarcasm.

I don't think she really knowed it but I was getting the feeling Penny was one of those know-it-alls.

"Back home, the deer and rabbits eat it," Fred added. He had some book learning, you could tell. I found it to be interesting especially with his background—his pa and all. I mean, heck, I didn't know all that about sassafras.

"My pa makes his own birch beer," I said. "Or at least he used to. I liked it right well."

"Oh, give me a Coca-Cola any day," said Penny. "Sure could go for one right about now."

"Let's go see what they got at the general store," Fred said.

"Don't they got no soda fountain in town?" asked Penny.

What was they talking about? I didn't have no money and I reckon they didn't neither, so I asked, "One of you fatheads got cash?"

They turned at me like I just said the dirtiest word they ever heard.

"No, we don't got no cash but we got pictures in our heads. You gotta lighten up, Breadline. You can't survive the jungles without some pretty pictures in your head."

Penny was right. I left home a dreamer but I got serious right quick and expectedly so.

I shrugged and made a face, "Guess it can't hurt to have a look-see. Besides, maybe one of them places will need some hired help."

"That's the spirit!" said Fred. "Let's go!"

We turned right on Market Street which brung us out just doors away from the general store. I couldn't help looking for Lou, and when I didn't see him, applied my "he can't see me" rule and followed the others. Penny walked straight-ways into the store but Fred stopped at one of the barrels in front. Now I had a chance to get a good look at him with his clothes on. He wasn't such a bad looking fella, though a little short for his age. Fred said he was fifteen and he sure was shorter than Penny, but then she was tall for a thirteen-year-old girl. Once I thought on it, I reckon most of the girls I knew back home was taller than the boys their age. He looked a might bit heavier when he was just wearing his under-clothes. In his jeans and stripy shirt he looked, well, not as ugly as he coulda been. But he had strange habits.

Fred lifted the barrel lid and stuck his head inside. I couldn't resist but come up behind him and poke his ribs.

"Ouch!" Fred yelped as he hit his head standing up with a start. "Not nice to scare a guy."

"Sorry," I said, somewhat laughing. "Whatcha got there."

"Pickles. Delicious crisp pickles. Wanna sniff?"

Fred commenced to breathing in long, slow breaths. Reminded me of sitting with a steaming bowl of water and a towel over my head when I had the cough and stuffed up head.

"Careful Fred, or one of them will get sucked up your nose and choke ya to death," I laughed, walking past him to the door.

"Aw, you don't know a good thing when you see it," he replied. "I can't buy 'em but I surely can imagine how they taste."

I didn't hear much else of what he said as I was already inside the store and feeling my little bit of heaven.

Nothing smells better than wood and plaster all mixed together with the smells of molasses and turpentine, at least not to me. I stood in the doorway taking it all in. Penny was already ogling the penny candy, and Fred was poking around a couple more barrels outside.

It was the last day of June and already warm, so the door was open when we come in. A light breeze blew through the store from a rear door just out of sight but I seen the daylight streaming across the old plank floor. Two long counters stretched down each side of the narrow store, and behind them from floor to ceiling was rows and rows of shelves stacked to the limit with dry goods, cloth, sacking, blankets, hat boxes, and hair tonics. Something, akin to a scrap of animal fur—but turned out to be a man's hairpiece—lay atop a wooden head on one of the shelves, as if ready to leap at unwary customers. Crates of nails and hammers, ropes, a stack of buckets, a bundle of mops and brooms, a barrel of tar, and other sundry items was scattered in seemingly sensible places around the two support posts located between the counters in the middle of the shop. A checkerboard with pieces already being played sat atop another barrel at which two stools was placed. The counter tops was littered with glove boxes, a glass jar filled with cigars, a humidor of pipe tobacco, a display of Lucky Strikes and Camels, another jar with combs, and a box of hair brushes. But of course, Penny had gravitated right to any kid's favorite place—the candy counter, where rows of glass jars held the treasures of childhood.

The store had a right good selection of candy for such a small town. There was not only peppermint sticks but many other flavors: cinnamon, cherry, red raspberry, grape. One jar held Mexican hat candies and another was filled with licorice sticks. The jars also held

Tootsie Rolls and the newer cellophane- wrapped hard candies, and a tall jar held a bundle of pretzel sticks. They kept the expensive candy bars like the Hersheys, Oh Henrys, and Bit O'Honeys, and the Paydays behind the counter just out of reach. Can't say I blamed them much for it. Them bars was a whole five cents apiece! But, my attention was drawn to the baseball cards with gum inside. I walked over to take a look, not that I had a collection, but I surely thought they was wonderful.

"Hey, look at this here," Penny said, pointing to a notice hanging just over the counter on the edge of one of the shelves. "Wanted, hardworking boy to sweep, stock shelves, and tend shop."

"Hey, you kids, mind what you handle unless you have cash money."

The man who run the shop appeared from the light I seen at the back. He musta been in the alley. He was brandishin' a broom.

"No monkey business, you hear!"

Penny tugged on my arm, "Come on, Blue, let's split. I can't stand the sight of all this candy and having no money to buy nothin'"

"You go on ahead," I told her, then I turned to the storekeep. "I seen this here notice, Mister. I reckon I'd like the job."

He looked me up and down. I was thinking I was mighty pleased we just bathed in the river.

"You look clean," he said. "You a vagrant? Never seen you around town."

"Well, sir, I reckon it depends on what you mean by vagrant."

"No back talk, boy. You got a home?"

"Um. Well, yessir, I do."

I knew he didn't mean my home back home but I didn't lie.

"That is, I have a home with a ma and pa if that's what you mean. I just ain't near it now. But I aim to stay here and work hard if you give me the job, at least until a week or two."

He hesitated, but I guess he liked the look of me because he tossed me a stock boy's coat and the broom.

"You start at six o'clock in the morning. Sweep the walk, wash the windows, and sweep the floor. Straighten up stock from the day before. If you find anything needs filling, you fill it with stock from the back room. You get lunch at noon and you finish at three. Lunch better be part of your pay by the looks of you, and you get five dollars a week and the room in the back to sleep."

I was grinning from ear to ear, then he added, "No handouts to nobody, not even your friends. It would be stealing, you hear?"

"Yessir!"

"And, they can sleep in the back too, only don't let on to my wife when she comes in."

"Yessir!"

"Now, get going. Your friends are waiting."

I fairly flew out the door but then I heard the man call me back. My heart sunk as I was surely thinking he changed his mind. Then I remembered I had his broom in my hands.

"I didn't get your name."

I walked back, a little red in the face for forgetting my manners. I leaned the broom against the wall and wiped my hand on my overalls.

"Blue . . . er, Billy, sir."

He took my hand and said his name was Mr. Willis.

"See you in the morning, Billy."

"Yessir!"

I looked up and down the street for Penny and Fred. They was on the other side of the green by then. *The green*. Last time I was there, Lou was chasing me down, but he was no place to be seen right then. I ran across the lawn and took a big leap.

"Yee Haw!" I shouted for the second time that day. "I got a job and we got us a place to spend the night!"

A Gold Stone

Penny and Fred was suspiciously silent over my good news. I let it drop, figuring maybe they wished they had asked for the work, and we continued our look about town. Fred stood outside the Five & Dime looking in the window all decked out in red, white, and blue for the upcoming holiday. It was the first time I noticed how the town had indeed changed overnight with many of the houses and shops decorated with flags and bunting. Red, white and blue bunting also hung on the town's gazebo.

"Reckon they'll have some fireworks?" I asked.

Fred wasn't listening. He was standing in the store's doorway.

"Are you going to stand there, son, or go inside?" said a man waiting to get past him. He was rude as he pushed past Fred.

Penny, who as it turned out was quite a scrapper, stepped forward with her fist raised.

"Hey Mister . . ." Her words was cut short as a policeman walked around the corner from the direction of the police station. He was whistling and swinging his stick. "goodday, officer," she added, changing her tune.

I pulled my cap over my eyes and sidestepped into a doorway left of the Five & Dime just as the officer tapped Penny on the shoulder with his stick. His face was stern.

"Move along, you two."

Penny and Fred obliged but in the opposite direction, leaving me standing in the doorway. Had it been a school day, we woulda been in a heap more trouble, but the officer had no cause but to walk by, that is until he spotted me loitering in the shadow of the doorway. He paused, putting the stick in the palm of his hand.

I quickly read the sign on the door. "Bar thol o mew Langston, D.D.S."

I stuck my tongue into my cheek to bulge it out and give a little groan as the policeman walked by. I mumbled something about a toothache and peeked from under my cap at him, and proceeded to open the door. The officer walked on by as I stepped inside the vestibule.

The vestibule was dark with a flight of wooden stairs directly in front and two glass-windowed office doors. The door on the right had a sign painted in black letters, it read "Mr. Jonathon Hanson, Attorney at Law" and the one on the left simply had a sign in the window saying "Goldstein, Jeweler." I seen a man bent over, working at a table in the jeweler's. I reckoned the dentist was straight on up the stairs. I smelled a familiar odor once before, when I went with my pa to have one of his teeth yanked out. The dentist called it "extraction" but it was "yanked," and there was no nicer word for it in my opinion. I heard my pa yelp clean out in the waiting room. I don't rightly know what makes the odor—chloroform or antiseptic or fear, or maybe a combination of all—but it was there wafting down the stairs. By now I took my tongue out of my cheek and was mighty happy I didn't really have a bad tooth. Then I heard the distant buzz of the dentist's drill and decided it was high-time to hightail it and see if I could find Penny and Fred. I caught up with them back over near the gazebo and we enjoyed my last day of freedom before I begun my new job. But the smell of the vestibule in the dental building stuck with me the rest of the day, at least until we made our way to the church on Market Street later in the afternoon.

By the time we got there, we was all three getting mighty hungry and Fred, who had been around town longer than Penny, knew they had a breadline for the poor just about suppertime. Sure enough, there was some tables set up outside the church to the right of the main entrance. They had some red and white checkered-tablecloths on the tables, a stack of bowls and spoons on the first table along with a big kettle, I reckoned was filled with soup. The middle tables held two or three platters with sandwich halves neatly stacked, and some paper plates. The third table held some Dixie Cups, some filled with water and others with Kool-Aid. The Ladies Auxiliary manned the tables and a line of destitutes had begun to form.

The line, which was longer than I thought it was going to be, was mostly men. There was at least one family with a mother and father and five children standing quietly—their faces deep and sunken, like they hadn't had no food in weeks. I seen Fred about to budge in line ahead of them when I grabbed him by the back of his suspender straps and give him a pull.

"Hey, what gives?" He shot me the evil-eye.

Just under my breath so as to save them the embarrassment, I said, "They was here first. 'Sides, we ate breakfast at the Army. Look at them folks, Fred. I doubt they seen any food in a long time." Fred's tension eased. "There's plenty of food."

"Yep," he said, bowing his head, a little ashamed of his over-exuberance. "Sorry 'bout that. I been gone so long, I reckon I don't got no manners no more."

I understood what he meant and give him a slap on the back. "You're a good man, Fred," I said.

The compliment made Fred smile. I reckon it woulda made me, too.

***

Penny, meantime, had struck up a conversation with one of the youngest of the five children—a little girl with red hair, almost as red as hers. In fact, Penny was just letting one of the girl's pigtails fall from her hand, when the mother turned around and took the child's hand to bring her back into line. I just caught the tip of what Penny said, "Don't never let nobody say it ain't pretty. It is."

The mother smiled at Penny and dragged her daughter in front of her so she could take a bowl from the lady who ladled the steaming soup.

"Vegetable with beef," the lady said, smiling at the mother like it was just another day on God's green earth.

I seen the sweet pity in the church-woman's eyes as the family passed by to the sandwiches. Now it was me standing in front of her, as Fred and Penny had become distracted by something happening in the line behind them.

"Good afternoon, son," the church lady said to me. "Would you like some soup, dear?"

"Yes'm."

I have always loved the sound of soup as it pours from the ladle into the bowl. It makes a sound like running water and then a gentle plop as each chuck of carrot, or potato—or in this case, a scrap of meat—falls into the broth. Now I was thinking of home again, wondering when I was ever going to be able to get some chicken soup to my pa. I was suddenly overcome by the foolishness of it all. Imagine asking the wife of the United States President to send me a pot of soup. What on earth had I been thinking?

The commotion at the rear of the line grew louder. It already had my companions' attention, and nobody could ignore it. A fight had broke out and it spilled from the walk into the street.

I couldn't resist grabbing two or three sandwiches and stuffing one in my mouth before pushing my way back through the breadline to find Penny and Fred. The whole back of the line had turned itself inside out in an effort to see what was going on. Fred was flushed with excitement as he told me what happened.

"That fella was just walking by when them five boys there grabbed him and started pushing him around." He shrugged when I asked why. "I didn't see him do nothing."

About eleven of the crowd—us three included—now formed a circle around the group of six boys, half on and half off the sidewalk and street. The rest of the folks waiting in line stood watching from a safe distance as if trying to determine whether they should still get their food or move on. The six boys was shouting and you could hear the sound of fists hitting flesh. Smack! Somebody threw a punch and sent the sixth boy—the one being attacked—flying. He landed on his back on the pavement. One of the other boys stood behind him like a wall to keep him from running, then picked him up and threw him back into the fight. I seen a spray of blood from his nose, and the boy who hit him laid into him again, this time running head-on at his gut.

"Get the Kike!"

"Jew boy!" another echoed. "Kike!"

By now, some of the men in line and from the church, and a few passers-by decided maybe they should try to break up the fight. Before they could do anything, two of the attackers latched onto the Jewish boy's arms and held him for a sucker punch. The bystanders trying to help, just got pulled into the fight or pushed out of the way. I pocketed the sandwich, grabbed Fred, and charged in.

Penny, like I said, was a scrapper. She was already clinging to a smaller boy's back, pounding him about the head. I think she may have even bit his ear, from the looks of it.

Fred and me raced in. I lost track of Fred but knew where I was heading. I crashed like a freight train into the boy who was head-butting, taking the Jew with me, then spun around to catch a blow upside the head.

"Five to one ain't fair!" I shouted at the top of my lungs. "Come on, cowards!"

I stood there breathing hard, blood already welling on my cheek. It was like the fight just ceased for a split second as one of the larger boys, obviously the ringleader, held out his arm to stop his friends. He stood right in the center of the street with his legs spread.

"Well boys, looks like we got us a Jew-lover here." Then he turned to me, "That right, boy? You a Jew-lover? Well, if you got any gold teeth, they ain't gonna be yours much longer because I'm gonna knock them clean out of your ugly face."

Not only the breadline folks but some town folks had gathered. People stood on nearby porches, and the church folk was trying to make some order out of the chaos. I give a quick glance to survey the situation. Penny had been dumped unceremoniously into a nearby garbage bin and I could see her fuming as she tried to pry herself free. Fred had another boy by the shoulders and the Jew was still behind me where he landed.Among the town folk was some kids with bicycles and two or three who looked like they was heading for a ball game. One was holding a baseball bat, and one of the attackers grabbed it out of his hands in one quick move and ran at us.

"Damn Jew-loving sons of bitches!"

He didn't get too far, as a leg was thrust out, sending him tumbling head over heels into the watching crowd. I couldn't believe my eyes.

"Pete!" I shouted. *It was Pete that tripped the bully! He wasn't dead! He didn't leave me!*

The scene right then reminded me of flip cards. You draw a picture on each card in a slightly different pose, then flip through 'em. Each picture looks like it's moving, and if you flip slowish, they move like slow motion. Well, it was like that. The motion started back up, only like it was one card flip at a time.

Pete come in rushing. Boys was running. Folks moved out of the way, so men from the crowd could run in and grab whoever they could catch. I heard the police whistle blasting and heard a siren—figured they brought a car and who knows—maybe a wagon. There was a scuffle and next thing I know, Pete had me by one arm, the Jew under his other, and Fred and Penny was scampering behind us.

Pete ducked us through the crowd and to the back door of the church. The nice church lady from the soup pot was there along with the sandwich lady. One held the door while the other watched outside for a minute.

"Hurry up now. Get yourselves in here," they said.

Once we was all inside, the sandwich lady closed the door and locked it behind her. Then she ran upstairs to the chapel to find out what was happening and to make sure nobody come down into the basement.

We was a sore-sight. Penny was pulling garbage out of her cap, hair, pockets, and even her ears. Fred and me was bruised and bleeding in at least a couple places. Pete had a scratch, but nothing compared to the gash healing on his left temple. And the Jew? Well, you almost couldn't tell there was a boy under all the blood. He musta been bleeding from every hole in his head, his arms, everywhere.

The nice soup lady, who said her name was Mrs. Wilma Johansson, took off her pretty silk jacket and put on an apron from the church kitchen. Then, she brung in a basin of warm water and some towels. Penny, me, and Fred took care of ourselves, but the Jewish boy sorely needed tending. He was barely conscious. Pete was checking his arms and legs for broken bones while Mrs. Johansson washed down his wounds. The clean water turned red mighty fast, and Fred was sent to the kitchen for more water. Penny was sent to wash herself up a bit.

"Is he gonna die?" I asked.

Pete give me a sharp glance. "Not yet," he replied.

Marilyn Smythe, the sandwich lady, come back down from the chapel with the news. Some of the other ladies of the church had taken over the breadline, and resumed serving. The townspeople had begun to leave and the police had settled the ruckus. Word was they caught the main instigator but the police wanted to question witnesses and was asking around for the other kids involved.

"I expect the boy's parents will be notified and nothing much will come of it except maybe a fine for using foul language in public. It's not the first time he's caused trouble," said Miss Smythe as she placed a tray of sandwiches and Kool-Aid on a table near the door. "You children never got any proper food from the line. Help yourself now. How is the boy?"

Mrs. Johansson replied, "I suspect he's going to hurt for quite a while but he is going to live. We need to find his family or at least call in the doctor."

Now, as she had wiped some of the dirt and blood away, the boy's face was easier to define. He had a shock of dark wavy hair. He weren't too tall, but tall enough to be about my age, sixteen. He was fairly well-dressed, though his clothes was probably going to be his work clothes from then on, all tore up as they was.

"Why, he's the jeweler's son. You know, that Jewish man who has the small jewelry shop in the dental building, the other side of the hall from Hanson. You know, by the Five & Dime," said Miss Smythe.

"Oh, yes," said Mrs. Johansson. "now, I see the resemblance. My Harold had his watch fob repaired there last month. I believe the family name is Goldstein. This must be young Rudolph Goldstein from my Elizabeth's class at school–such a quiet boy. I wonder what caused this attack."

"Why, Wilma, you know as well as I do there is a faction in this town who just can't stand the sight of Jews. I reckon the Hanson boy did not act on his own."

Hanson. I knew the name. I seen it that very day. Then it come to me. "You talking about the lawyer, Hanson?"

The boy moaned.

"He's coming to," said Pete, who had been listening in to everything the ladies had to say. "We can send one of the kids to get his father. Which one of you two wants to go?" He was looking at Fred and Penny.

"I can go," I spoke up. "I know right where to find his shop."

Pete leaned over so I could hear him but not everyone else could. "I need you to stay with me. Trust me on this."

Fred volunteered saying it was better for him than Penny, just in case some of the gang was still lurking about.

"Wait!" shouted Pete. "Take this, so he'll know."

It was the boy's cap. Fred took off to fetch Mister Goldstein.

"Get him some water," Pete ordered, but Miss Smythe already had a glass in hand. She give it to Pete, then went back upstairs to keep watch.

"Take small sips, son," Pete said as he tipped the glass. To us he added, "No use you two just hanging around. Get yourselves some of the extra sandwiches from the tray while you can. Once Mr. Goldstein gets here, we'll figure out what to do next."

Penny and me didn't have to be told twice and we helped ourselves to the sandwiches, washing them down with Kool-Aid almost as soon as we took a bite. Of course, I ate the now-smashed sandwich from my pocket first.

Fred musta run into the doc before he got to Goldstein's shop, or else the doctor had the inclination he might be needed, because he arrived before anyone sent for him.

The town doctor was an older gentleman, much older than my pa by the looks of the grey streaks in his hair. He wore gray suit pants and a white shirt with the top button undone as it was a hot day—black socks and shoes. He was right proper, except for the lack of a suit coat or hat. His sleeves was rolled up against the heat.

By the time the doctor arrived, the boy was awake and sitting up, leaning against a wall and alert enough to tell us his name was indeed Rudolph—only he said it was Rudy. I knew enough from overhearing Pete and Mrs. Johansson to know Rudy was the shortened name for Rudolph. Rudy and his pa come from Germany. Doc said, Rudy's ma died short-time after he was born. From all I heard in the fight, they was Jews and Jews weren't much liked by some folk, much like the colored folk. But it wasn't nothing to me, short, fat, colored, white, Jew or not, I always reckoned a fella's behavior spoke louder. Reckon it was what my folks taught me. Surely felt sorry for Rudy right then. He was a mess of cuts and bruises, and from what the doc said, mighty lucky we stepped in when we did.

Now, the doc seemed like a nice enough fella, but Pete and me both agreed he was likely to make a report to the law, which was bad for us, and for Penny and Fred too. As soon as we was sure Rudy was in good hands, when Fred returned, we stuffed Pete's satchel with some sandwiches and a jar of pickles Mrs. Johansson found in the kitchen. I returned the satchel to him gratefully, and then we lit out for the water tower just south of town.

The sun was already setting and we could see the glow of several small fires as we neared the tower. Crossing the railroad tracks running between town and the river, we come to a hobo jungle. It was not the same one Mack and Lou had, this one was bona fide.

From what I could tell, Penny and Fred and Pete had all been there before. They was fairly popular, as quite a few "regulars" greeted them as we entered.

Fred led us straight to a shelter under the tower and threw himself down. "Man, it's good to be home."

It struck me kinda hard just how much I left back in Wellsboro. I had a ma and a pa, leastwise I prayed my pa was still among the living. Here was Penny with no kin to care what happened to her and no place to go except to find her aunt and see if she could get a handout. Then there was Fred who had kin but was abused and laid his head wherever he threw hisself down. Pete? I still didn't know much about him. And Rudy. His bloodied face, and the thought of how much his pa was going to worry on him, stuck with me all the time after that day. I recalled the ladies said his last name was Goldstein. I later found out Goldstein meant gold stone and I thought it was a might queer since I never knew him at all but he changed my life in profound ways. He would be my gold stone—my lucky piece.

See, none of the folks I met did nothing to harm nobody and yet they all had their share of hardships. Life ain't fair. Lord, I hear people talk about fairness all the time and complain about what they ain't got, but I never once heard any of *these* folks say it. No sir, they weren't alive for fairness. They was alive because they could be, and knew every single day could be the last. Yeah, every single day could be the last. I was sure there was something in the wind for me.

I sat with my friends by their fire and shared some pickles. I have to say I truly took pleasure in watching Fred pucker up after all the talk at the pickle barrel. We talked about our adventures and how it seemed like a week and not a day, and how we felt like we knowed each other all our lifetimes. Penny sang her favorite song, Pennies From Heaven—no surprise there. Then Pete took me aside.

"Billy," he paused and thought a minute. "No, Blue. You said your friends call you Blue and I think we're friends. I owe you an explanation about what happened with Mack and Lou and maybe who I am. You see, that night at Mack's camp, they came over while we were sleeping and kicked me awake. I know we meant not to sleep, but well, we did. Those two started accusing me of being a detective and spying on their operations. They thought so because of my manner of carrying myself, and my speech. Well they were wrong, and when they couldn't find any proof, it didn't matter. They decided they couldn't leave me alive now that I knew they were up to something."

I interrupted. "They're bank robbers, aren't they?"

"More than that Blue, they've also been crisscrossing the state following payrolls. It's only a matter of time before they get found out because, you see, I am quite alive, and I turned them in. I gave a full description of them and their operations to the police in town."

I give a low whistle knowing what it meant for them and for Pete.

"But what happened to you, Pete? You disappeared and I admit, I thought you was dead."

"Well, so did they. Lou and the other fella, Hank is his name, they roughed me up good and conked me over the head with a pistol butt. Next thing I knew, I woke tangled in the root of a tree that was fallen across a narrow branch of the river. They threw me in to drown but those roots turned me over and held me fast until I woke. Once I freed myself and cleared my head, I doubled back to find you, but you weren't in sight."

"I was out cold in Mack's shack for at least five days."

"That explains it. Anyway, today was the first time I saw any trace of you and I followed until I was sure Mack and Lou didn't have you. Then the fight started."

Pete was like the older brother I never had. I plum forgot myself for a moment and threw my arms around him, and I reckon I cried some.

"Oh Pete, I'm . . . " I stepped back wiping my eyes. "I'm glad you're alive. I got a job in town at the general store, Pete. Gonna work at least a week and then we can hop a train again. I'm still heading for D.C."

Suddenly, I recalled I had a good place for us all to spend the night and the hour was getting late.

"Hey, I gotta run. I gotta get to the store for the night and you all can come. Mr. Willis said so."

The air changed. What felt warm and joyful suddenly felt drafty and glum.

"Well, what's the matter with y'all? You looking your noses down at a decent place to sleep?"

Fred stood and Penny walked over to Pete and me.

"Didn't Fred tell ya, Breadline?" Penny asked. "We're leaving on the midnight train, southward bound."

"Pete?" I asked, looking at him, and trying to maintain my composure.

"Sorry, Blue. Me too. I didn't plan it this way, but now I know you're safe, and I have business elsewhere that needs attention. See, I never told you all about me, and I'm not about to tell it all now, but I had a business once—a good one—and my old partner is in Atlanta. When I first met you in Wellsboro under the bridge, I felt like a defeated man, but Blue . . . " Pete put his hand firm on my shoulder. "I don't understand it, but when I thought maybe Mack and Lou had done you harm, I decided not to waste my life in the past but to find a way to build it up again, and then I planned to go visit your folks. You'll see me again someday. I promise."

Pete reached inside his vest pocket and took out his gold pocket watch. He flipped it open and read the time.

"10:30. You better get a move on, Blue. You have a job waiting in the morning."

Then he took my hand and stuck the watch in my palm.

"Remember, Blue, "Veni vidi vici."

Through the tears, I managed to say, "I came. I saw. I conquered."

"You keep it for me, Blue."

"I can't take your watch."

"You can hand it back to me someday, but for now . . . "

I think Pete mighta had a tear in his eye, as he turned so I couldn't see. After a hug from Penny and a handshake from Fred, we all promised to take care of ourselves. I promised Pete I'd stay clear of Mack and Lou and the Hanson gang, and then I set out on a slow walk back to the store.

There was a full moon and I guess I wiped tears most of the way, while trying to read the pocket watch in the moonlight. The side door to Willis's store was still unlocked and a soft light glowed in the back room. There was a glass of milk and a biscuit, and a note beside the snack. *Lock up, get some sleep. Six in the morning. Mr. Willis.*

I lay my head on the soft feather pillow left by Mrs. Willis and the low ticking of Pete's watch lulled me to sleep. Maybe sometime around midnight, I woke for one brief moment to the sound of a train. *Whoooo!* And I said a silent goodbye to friends I doubted I'd ever see again.

July 1-4, 1937
Independence

Working for Mr. Willis kept me right busy. I'm no shirker but after three eight-hour days, I was ready for the holiday festivities.

I met plenty of kind folks from the town who come in to do business and they didn't seem to mind when I had to wait on them. I even recalled some of their names, and the regulars already took to calling me Blue.

In those three days, I never once seen hide nor hair of the Hanson kid, but I did hear once or twice some people talking about what happened in the breadline. They said the police had questioned the boy and set him free to the custody of his pa, the lawyer, and they was still looking for the other kids involved in the fight for questioning. Mr. Willis said, in no uncertain terms, the Hanson boy and his gang of wild animals was not allowed to set foot in his store. I took him seriously.

Mr. Willis told me he would dock my pay five cents a day so I could help myself to some food put up for me by Mrs. Willis. It was good eating and five cents for three meals a day was worth it. I took my meals across the street in the green. I must say it was enjoyable to have some eating time just to watch the town folk go about their daily routines. Just two days back, the local wise guys was already setting off firecrackers everywhere in town. Seems like hardly an hour went by you didn't hear Crackle! Pop! Thursday, a boy come 'round the store with a stack of poster signs under his arm asking if he could hang one in Mr. Willis' window. Willis said yes and handed it to me to hang. The sign said there was going to be a social in the park on the afternoon of the Fourth, followed by fireworks off the island.

Fair excitement was everywhere, just like the sound of them firecrackers. Small towns just live from one celebration to the next, and in Selinsgrove, it seemed doubly so because they had only one moving picture show, unlike some of the larger cities. They also had laws saying exactly when you could buy liquor and forbidding drinking of it outside the home or drinking establishment. The only other public pastime, except for the Tuesday band at the gazebo, was a pool hall and beer joint, but respectable folks stayed away from that side of the tracks.

***

Willis' General Store was closed on Sunday, July Fourth. Most of the town musta gone to church at the Lutheran on Market Street, but I seen a few automobiles heading on north toward the bridge to any number of churches in Sunbury, or else west to Middleburg and the United Church of Christ. Then of course, there was those who didn't go to church. Mama called them heathens. I got to wondering if Jews went to church and what Mama would call them if they didn't, because Rudy didn't seem at all heathen by my definition. The Hansons, Mack, and Lou—now they was worse than heathens as far as I was concerned. As for the hobos down by the river, I was mighty curious what they did on the Sabbath, but after I got to thinking on it, I was able to answer my own question. Why would they go to church? They really had no home or roots. I was probably the only one who stayed put this long, and what respectable church would want many of the poor fellas I seen in the jungle? Most likely not a one, but then I was an unusual case. I found out right quick when the Willises showed up at the store to take me to church. I protested a heap, saying I only had the clothes on my back, but Mrs. Willis insisted.

"The good Lord didn't care at your home so why would he care here? He's the same God," she said.

I was a bit nervous about the church, seeing how last time I been there, I was bleeding in the street and watching Rudy bleeding in the basement, but people tend to turn a blind eye on Sunday in the Lord's house. We walked right in the front door.

The Willises took a bulletin from the usher's hand and turned to me.

"I believe you've met my stock boy . . ."

Mr. Willis started to introduce me as Billy, which of course is my name, but Mrs. Willis interrupted, "William." Then she smiled at me right pretty, took my hand like I was a little boy, and proceeded down the aisle in front of Mr. Willis.

It was a might uncomfortable and my cheeks got all hot. I gingerly slid my hand away, as I slicked back my hair the best I could and looked at the floor hoping nobody had seen me. I heard a girl giggle and seen her from the corner of my eye. She wasn't watching what happened with my hand but rather pointing to another girl to look at my ankles. I didn't have no socks and the pant legs on my overalls was a tad shorter than the fashion, on account I had a growth spurt since Mama bought 'em last fall. I couldn't wait to find our seat, but sadly, it was in the third row from the front, and the walk took forever.

"You slide in first, dear," Mrs. Willis said. Her voice was so kindly, I reckon she woulda charmed the skin off a possum and there was just no doing anything against her will. Now I knew why Mr. Willis said not to tell her he had invited Penny and Fred to sleep in the shop. If she didn't approve of something, then it wasn't happening. I did as she said, then she slid in beside me, and

Mr. Willis sat on the end. By the time we did all this, the organ was already playing the opening hymn "Nearer My God to Thee" and without even opening the hymnal, Mrs. Willis was belting it out just like Mama used to. I smiled apiece to myself and sang along, only not as loud.

Truth be told, I enjoyed church, the singing and the organ. They was upliftin', and for a little while, Pa's sickness and the worry in Ma's eyes and all the troubles of the past few weeks melted away into one dream. The church-folks wasn't too bad neither.

Just as I thought, Hanson and his son was not in church. Well, maybe they went over to one of the other churches in the County. All I know was I was right glad they weren't in the Willises' church. That nice Mrs. Johansson and Miss Smythe was there, and they asked on Rudy and the others. Miss Smythe said she hadn't noticed my eyes the other day but they was "Blue as the sky." I thanked her, and remembered Penny's hair and kind of understood why she didn't like folks making a fuss over it.

I had to tell the ladies I hadn't seen none of my friends since the other day, putting it in my head that maybe I should stop 'round Goldstein's jewelry and ask on Rudy myself.

As soon as me and the Willises touched the sidewalk, I thanked them for church and told them I would see them at the social later but I had to pay a call. I headed straight-ways toward the dental building.

Of course the Five & Dime was closed, as was the offices in the dental building. I suppose I hoped Mr. Goldstein—who didn't celebrate on Sunday—mighta been there workin'. I stood, cupping my eyes with my hands, to see into the main door window as the door was locked.

I couldn't help wondering what it musta been like for Mr. Hanson to walk past Goldstein's jewelry everyday knowing, it was run by a Jew. His son sure didn't get the way he was without help from his father. And hadn't the ladies at the church also said they doubted he acted alone? That there was a faction in town? Well now I wondered about the faction and got to thinking it might be the KKK—the Ku Klux Klan. They hated colored folk and Jews and all manner of other folks just for being different from themselves. Shoot, I was different from some folks and some folks was different from me, and I reckon I liked it. I guess I always thought a little different, too. Just having these thoughts was different from lots of folks. I can't really imagine a world where everybody acts and thinks alike.

I couldn't see no lights on in the building, and the street window of Goldstein's was dark. There was always a chance he wouldn't be there, but I never expected to find what I did. There was a sign in the window on the inside door and I could make out what it said. It didn't say, "Closed." It read "Out of Business."

My heart sank. Deep down inside, I really had been hoping someone would be there so I could ask about Rudy. What would make such a prominent jeweler close up for good? I knew Mrs. Johansson's husband used his services and I figured lots of folks did since he was the only jeweler in town. But then, I reckon I knew the answer. It was Hanson. I knew if I had the stuffing beat out of me the way Rudy did, to the point of almost dying, my pa would have done the same. No use sticking around where you ain't wanted, and I doubted it was a first time for the Goldsteins. I disliked Hanson a might more, right about then.

There's nothing much to do on a Sunday morning in Selinsgrove, Pennsylvania, so I wandered down to the river where I found another sad sight. The jungle where Fred and Penny had lived before hopping the train had been cleared out. Turns out they have to clear them out every Independence Day so folks have a place to sit and watch the fireworks, but the 'bos always move back in once the celebration is over. I crossed a small bridge to the island and hung around, watching some men set up their fireworks displays, though they wouldn't let me get too close. I found an old fishing pole one of the 'bos had left behind in the move and did me a little fishing, too. The last couple days was like a life of luxury for me, even with working, and that's a fact. 'Round about three o'clock–by Pete's pocket watch, I headed on back to town for the social.

I reckon Wellsboro had such socials, but Ma and Pa and me, we lived more rural and without the truck which Pa and me had to put on the blocks, well, going into town as a family wasn't so easy. Sure, I went to sit in the barbershop and listen to the old cronies, but it was about the only time unless Mama needed something at the store, which was rarely. So if Wellsboro had socials, I never knew. I had no idea what to expect and was surely pleased when I found out. Summertime is fresh strawberry time and this here was a strawberry social.

If it had strawberries in it, you could find it there. They had strawberry preserves, strawberry pie, strawberry cake, strawberry ice cream, and best of all strawberry shortcake–a plate with a nice flaky home-baked powder milk biscuit piled high to overflowing with mashed strawberries and cream. Oh my Lord, it was heaven. Many of the town's ladies had entered their home-baked goods in a contest, including Mrs. Willis. I knew her biscuits as soon as I seen them, and I made good and sure my shortcake was made with her biscuits. Of course, I had to ask Mr. Willis for a small advance on my week's pay which he give me right willingly. I only took fifty cents though. I didn't want to spend it all. I still needed some things for the rest of my journey to Washington.

After I ate my shortcake, I wandered over to watch the Selinsgrove Independence Day Parade. I hid behind a few folks so as not to be too out in the open. There was a contingent of police and firefighters leading the way, the high school band, the local veteran's group, the Salvation Army band, and I seen that pretty Sister Sarah with her hair still up in the bun. And there was kids with their bicycle spokes and handlebars decked out in red, white, and blue crepe paper streamers. They even had the Selinsgrove Strawberry Princess. She was Mrs. Johansson's daughter Elizabeth, who went to school with Rudy. Mrs. Johansson was at the social and told me after the parade when everybody milled about the green.

"That's my Elizabeth. Isn't she pretty, Billy? Have you ever seen a prettier girl?"

"No Ma'am," I said, and I wasn't lying neither. She was right pretty—prettier than any girl I ever seen before, except maybe some of them Hollywood starlets from the magazines in the store.

I musta been all agog because I never heard Mrs. Johansson ask, "Would you like to meet my Elizabeth, Billy?"

"What, Ma'am? Oh . . ." It was at that very moment the lovely Selinsgrove Strawberry Princess come drifting across the lawn toward her mama. "Ma'am?"

"Would you like to meet her?"

I didn't know what to say, and there was no need. Mrs. Johansson had already been swept up in a whirl of white and soft pink crinoline, the scent of strawberries made me dizzy and I gone all white.

"Ma'am, I don't reckon I'm feeling right well," I begun to say, but the white and pink cloud was standing right before me, her soft chestnut hair falling around the angel's face and soft green eyes looking deep into my very soul.

"Elizabeth, this here is Mr. Willis' stock boy, Billy."

"Oh," said the angel. "The boy who had the fight with John Hanson?"

Lord, I wish she didn't know I was in a fight, but she didn't seem to mind. She was all smiles, and a soft hand stuck out to shake mine. I just stared at her hand forever it seemed.

"I'm pleased to meet you, Billy."

I finally touched her hand but I didn't want to squeeze like I did the boys. Sad to say my palms was sweating too.

"My friends call me Blue."

Really? Was that all I could manage? Here was the sweetest, most beautiful angel I ever seen and probably ever would see, and all I could say was "Call me Blue"?

"Pleased, Blue."

I think I managed a smile, though later I found myself looking in every shiny mirror or window I could find and testing my smile to see what I must have looked like to her. It was plum tragic.

"I have to go get ready for the judging, Mama," Elizabeth said. Then off floated *my cloud.*

Like I said, I spent the rest of the afternoon practicing my smiles, watching the judging, and pretending the Strawberry Princess was waving just at me. I ate as much strawberry shortcake as fifty cents will buy and had enough left over to buy some firecrackers off a kid who was reluctant to hand them over until he seen I was paying for them.

Suddenly, out of the corner of my eye, I seen a familiar pair of tan trousers, plaid shirt, and tan fedora working through the people in the park. It was Lou, and not far behind him was Mack and Hank, and a few other fellas I seen that night in the jungle. It was time to skedaddle and make myself scarce.

On the Road Again

I had no doubt Mack and his boys was up to something illicit, and I just couldn't risk being spotted. Diving down one of the alleys, I went looking for the Willises, as I thought I might go back to the shop but it would be locked. Since I slept in the back room of the store, there was no reason for Mr. Willis to give me a key and I liked it that way. With fewer responsibilities in case somebody got in who shouldn't, I couldn't be blamed.

I found the Willises walking up the street in the direction of a tree, over in front of the Five & Dime.

"Mr. Willis!" I called.

They turned and waited for me to cross the street.

"Are you enjoying the day, William?" asked Mrs. Willis.

I nodded and was about to ask Mr. Willis my question when our attention was drawn to the tree and the crowd forming at its base. It had to be the biggest tree I ever seen. If three growed men took hands, they couldn't reach all ways around it. Mr. Willis said the tree was there since the town was founded in 1787 by a man name of Selin who fought with George Washington in the Revolutionary War. Heck, I thought maybe he even planted that tree. The tree was a sycamore towering over the Five & Dime, with one long limb hanging out over the roof.

I did make sure I was well-hid amongst the crowd now forming at the base of the tree. For now, Mack and the others was nowhere in sight, and I was grateful. "What's going on?"

It wasn't the question I had planned to ask but it made sense at the moment, since the peaceful Sunday social looked more like a curious mob right then.

Mr. Willis pointed up in the tree and I followed his gesture. Mrs. Willis was nearly shaking.

"That fool boy is going to get himself killed," she said. "Where are his parents?"

Mr. Willis ignored her question as he turned to me.

"He's a tree-sitter, Billy. See the sign and box there at the base of the tree?"

Sure enough, it was there. The sign said "David MacDonald will sit in this here tree longer than anybody. Donations welcome." And there was some coin building up in the box.

"Why is he up there?" I asked.

"Well, Billy, I guess we're doing such good business at the general store, the Five & Dime needs to advertise. See, they put their name on the sign."

I hadn't read far enough. I looked back at the sign and along the bottom, and it did indeed say "Sponsored by Folaron's Five & Dime. Come in and shop."

"I didn't think they could be open on Sunday," I said.

"They're not open, Billy. Looks like this kid decided today was a good day to start his tree-sitting, while there was a crowd gathered. He's making some good money."

"How long you figure a boy can stay up in a tree?" I asked.

A man standing next to Mrs. Willis leaned toward us and said "Ten days, son. A man over in Sunbury just finished sitting for ten days, and I once heard about a kid they called Rhubarb who sat for one hundred seven days!"

"You mean they sleep up there?"

"They sure do. Sleep, eat, and no toilet or bath. Just a bucket on a rope for sending food and water up and another for nature's call. I seen one man get a haircut from the barber in a tree once. I don't think I woulda trusted the barber to have a steady hand up there. He was shaking worse than the leaves."

This was when Mrs. Willis said she had enough of our foul talk and waste of time and took both Mr. Willis and me by the arms.

"Did you both have enough to eat?"

We nodded. Mr. Willis was smiling like the devil with a twinkle in his eye. I think he kind of liked teasing on the missus.

"Then it's time for us to get some chairs to take down to the river for the fireworks, don't you think so?" she added.

Like I said, there was no arguing with Mrs. Willis. They sent me back to the store with the key to fetch the chairs while they went to a street vendor around the corner. It all worked out since I wanted to go fetch my things anyway.

When I showed up with the chairs and my bundle, Mr. Willis handed me an open bottle of Coca-Cola. Once we found a spot Mrs. Willis agreed to and sat ourselves down, I just let the beverage slide down my throat. Ice cold and so wonderful. I was in my heavenly days until I remembered why I had gone looking for the Willises.

"Mr. Willis?"

"Yes, Billy?"

"I was meaning to ask you for, well, for a favor and some advice."

It seemed to me, in those few days, the Willises had started thinking of me like their son, who died in the last war. It weren't like I needed a family, I had one—but I must admit, it was nice knowing I made them somewhat happy. I knew what I was going to say would break Mrs. Willis' heart.

"Sir," I swallowed. "I been working for three days now, and I had hoped to stay at least the week, maybe two."

I seen Mrs. Willis shoot her husband a glare.

"Jonathan."

He patted her hand.

"We, Betsy and I . . . " He looked at her from the corner of his eye. "We understand you were on your way someplace. We had hoped you'd change your mind. You're a good worker."

"Thank you," I said, "but I was on my way to Washington to get help for my folks and only needed to make enough money to buy a few things like food. You been real kind folks and maybe I will pass this way again, but something has come up and I mean to light out tonight."

Mrs. Willis got up out of her chair and walked off a pace.

"Don't mind her, Billy. She'll be all right. What do you need from me?"

"Well, sir, I got a piece of important business I have to do in town and then I reckon it won't be good for me being here after that."

"You in some kind of trouble, son?"

"No, sir," I replied. "Leastwise, not of my own doing, but I do have to go to the police station."

Mr. Willis had a mighty serious look on his face.

"So you want your pay for the week and for me to walk to the station house with you?"

"No, sir, just the pay due me for the three days and I can see my own way to the station. Nice folks like you and Mrs. Willis shouldn't get caught up in this. It wouldn't be right."

"All right, son, if you're sure there isn't another way. You've proven yourself to be a good hard working young man and we couldn't have been prouder of our own son. I'll pay you your wages, but Mrs. Willis will never speak to me again if she knew I let you go to the police alone. It's the way it is."

I had to shake on it. His hand was firm and not going anywhere unless I did. He reached in his pocket and peeled three dollars off a roll of bills.

"This is more than we agreed, sir."

"Well, if you expect me to make exact change, Billy, you are asking too much." There was that twinkle in his eye again.

By then, Mrs. Willis had walked off, completely out of sight. I took the dollars and tucked them inside the bib of my overalls.

"I'd surely like to say goodbye to the missus."

"Billy. Uh, Blue . . . "

It was the first time Mr. Willis had called me Blue. I knew it meant he accepted what was and he thought on me as a friend.

"Blue, sometimes, goodbye doesn't need to be said. And Mrs. Willis knows you are grateful for everything she did for you. I think she would like best just to hear from you sometime, saying you are well."

I stood to go on over to the police station.

"And, Blue?"

"Yes, sir."

"I wouldn't mind hearing, too."

He smiled and put his arm around my shoulder, and we walked back to town like father and son, or two good friends.

By the time we arrived at the police station, most of the townsfolk was already down by the river. I had no way of knowing where Mack and his gang was slinking about. As we walked, I explained to Mr. Willis what happened and how Pete had already gone to the police about Mack and Lou, but apparently the police had not picked them up yet. I told him how I expected they was up to no-good while everybody was busy with the celebrations and that once I told the police, because of my run-in with Hanson, I would have to light out right quick. Mr.

Willis understood, though he did say he would vouch for me. Mostly, I was concerned about getting on to Washington.

The small station was manned as it was all the time, but with only two on-duty police still at the station house. The others was patrolling the river banks to make sure folks was safe. Even with so little happening, we was asked to take a seat and wait. Nobody else was there except a raggedy fella being booked for loitering and public drunkenness.

It was already getting dark outside.

"Mr. Willis, the fireworks will be starting soon. Don't you want to go be with Mrs. Willis?"

"It is quite all right, Blue. If I were to go back without helping you, I would be sleeping in the backroom tonight."

"Okay folks, what can I do for you?" The officer at the desk called us over. He looked at Mr. Willis waiting for his complaint.

"No," said Mr. Willis, "it isn't me. It's the boy."

"Vagrant?"

Mr. Willis paused. "No, he is an employee—my stock boy. He had a run-in . . . "

"Excuse me, sir," I interrupted. It was my story to tell and I wanted to leave Mr. Willis out of it as much as I could. "I'd like to report some men who is taking advantage of boys and up to no-good."

The officer had a complaint form out on his desk. The officer cleared his throat and looked up over his spectacles at me.

"Name?"

"Mack and Lou."

"No, son, he wants *your* name," said Mr. Willis.

"Oh, well, um . . ." I didn't want to give my true name but I wouldn't lie neither.

"His name is William Willis." Mr. Willis lied through his teeth but I heard him mumble under his breath, "Mostly."

"Age?"

"Sixteen, almost seventeen," I said.

"And what is the nature of your complaint?"

I hesitated and now the officer was looking at me.

"Your complaint?" the officer repeated.

"Well, sir, there are these two men. They call themselves hobos, but they ain't . . . um, are not. They're rough with boys they find and make them do terrible things."

The officer was unmoved but listened.

"Such as?"

"Well, sir, they make them be Angelinas. You know what I mean, right?" I was glad when he nodded. "And they hold things against them to make them do what they say. Make them rob people. My friend Pete told you about them two—Mack and Lou. I don't know no . . . er, I don't know any last names, but they hang out in a jungle west of town, only it ain't...isn't, a bona fide jungle, sir. It's a hideout for the gang, and sir, I seen them in town at the social, acting all suspicious. They're up to something. That's why I come and told you."

The officer was scribbling notes as fast as I could talk. He only looked up again when I said Mack's and Lou's names. Mr. Willis couldn't believe what he was hearing, even though I told him on the way there. I reckon it was pretty hard information, especially when I told the policeman I knowed it because I was one of them boys.

"Okay, son," the officer said. "I got it all here. I recall your friend Pete but we can't just haul in everybody a man says is doing something. We need hard, cold evidence. But in your case, son, you are a minor and a victim of these men. This may be all we need."

Now he was looking at Mr. Willis.

"I will need your address and telephone number. Your boy is a witness and may be called to testify."

I stiffened at the idea and shot Mr. Willis a worried look. I didn't need to say nothing. He knew what it meant.

"Is that absolutely necessary?" asked Mr. Willis.

"Well, unless we catch them red-handed in the act of committing a crime, it is. If you want to press charges."

Mr. Willis give him the information he needed, thanked him, then nodded me toward the door. Once outside, I told him, "I am sure they're planning something tonight during the fireworks and it will be all the police need, but I can't stick around long enough to testify."

"I know. Though, I wish you would stay the night," he said. "There's a train in the morning but tonight the closest train heading south toward Washington is over in Sunbury."

"No, sir, Mr. Willis, I think it best if I leave tonight."

"Well, then at least let me drive you over."

"Out of all due respect I kept you away from Mrs. Willis long enough and I don't want to be a burden."

"It isn't a burden if someone offers, Blue."

"Just the same, sir, I reckon leaving now is best and going alone will give me some time to think. I got plenty to think on."

He was reluctant but held out his hand and I took it. Like I said, he had a good solid handshake, but he pulled me in for a fatherly hug and pat on the back.

"If you ever come back this way, Blue, if you need a job, you come see me. You hear?"

I thanked him and we walked together as far as the corner of Pine and Market.

"Take Market and just keep following the river north until you come to the bridge, Blue. Then stay on Market until you come to the water tank near the tracks. There should be a train through there near midnight. Take care of yourself."

"I will, sir," I said but I felt my eyes getting all watered up again. I didn't look back to see if he was watching or if he had gone on back to the river. It was dark by then, and just as I rounded the corner, I heard the first muffled sound of fire-works taking to the air followed by a heart-thudding BOOM and then crackle. Now I looked back and seen the sparks floating down to earth. I was getting tired of always moving on. I did have some thinking to do.

Midnight Special

The walk to Sunbury was about five miles and would only take two hours, give or take in the dark. By the look of the pocket watch, it was nearly ten, and I would just make the midnight train on time. Still I was grateful for a truck coming down the road just about a half-mile outside town, so I stuck out my thumb. The truck slowed, and I could see a man and woman, most likely goin' home after the social in Selinsgrove but not staying for the fireworks. Looking over my shoulder, I seen the bright colors sparkling in the sky behind me. Ahead at Sunbury, I could almost make out their fireworks too, since the sky was so clear, with the moon and stars being the only light.

"Where you heading, son?" the man asked, the woman leaning back so he could speak across her.

"Just to Sunbury," I told him.

"Hop in the back."

I tipped my cap. "Much obliged."

They waited for me to hop in, but when I did, there was already another fella sitting there. He moved over so I could fit, then knocked on the truck bed to tell them I was in. The truck lurched as the driver shifted into gear, and I rocked back on my bottom. The stranger took hold of the wooden truck rail with one hand and my overalls' strap with the other.

"Hang on there, son," he said. He looked me over, and seeing my bindle asked, "You riding the train out of Sunbury?"

"I expect to," I replied.

"Well, if you have to get a topside-seat . . . " He shifted himself to give me more room. "That is, if you have to ride on top of the train instead of in a car, it's going to be way more bumpy than this. You'll get clean thrown off going around the slightest turns if you aren't holding on."

"Thank you," I said, realizing how fortunate I had been so far. I had help navigating my way through difficult situations at almost every step. I think Mama would feel a might easier if she knew I had help.

"Naples is the name. Tom Naples."

I shook his hand and introduced myself.

"Folks call me . . . " I thought on it a moment and then remembered the nickname Penny give me. "Breadline Blue, that's what they call me."

"Well, you can call me Tom. Should I call you Breadline or Blue for short?"

"I expect 'Blue' is what most folks use."

"Well, Blue, it's good to share the ride, though I wish this old truck had better springs."

I laughed. "You figuring on taking the train?" I asked, expecting him to say yes.

"No, Blue, I'm just traveling from town to town looking for work. The trains take me too far off from where I need to be. Besides, it's hard hauling this here guitar and hopping the trains."

Tom reached behind hisself and lifted the neck of his guitar case so I could see.

"So, you're a musician?"

"I play a might, and find it very interesting to meet people and see new places. You ever hear of a fella named Woody Guthrie?"

"Nope."

I don't reckon I ever seen a growed man get so excited over a singer, though Mama surely got herself in an uproar over hearing

Bing Crosby when the radio was working right. Tom fairly spit out his excitement.

"Blue, I'm telling you, this Guthrie is quite the singer and songwriter. I just come back from California and he is on the radio out West. He's been writing songs about the everyday man, the poor folks, and he's causing quite a stir. He sings about the unions too. He writes from someplace deep in his soul and you can't help but get worked up. I'm back here now, singing and trying to let folks know what's happening out West, and letting them hear Woody's music."

The ride was too bumpy to expect Tom to play his guitar but he could really sing a lick. He talked about one of Woody's songs called *This Land is Your Land*, and he sung a couple other songs that surely stirred my blood and made me think I was doing the right thing by my folks. One was called *I Ain't Got No Home.*

I ain't got no home
I'm just a rambling 'round
A hard-working man
I roam from town to town
And the police make it hard wherever I may go
And I ain't got no home in this world anymore.

I must say, the song that I thought was the prettiest and brung a tear to my eye was one Tom said Woody didn't write, but was singing and people was listening. It was *Hobo's Lullaby.*

Go to sleep, you weary hobo
Let the towns go drifting by
Can't you hear the steel rails hummin'
That's the hobo's lullaby.

I was downright homesick then. I wiped my eyes and sniffled, I reckon.

"That's the most rightful truth, Tom," I said.

"And Woody is making changes happen, Blue. If a man can sing, he can make people listen."

"You reckon it's true if a man can speak, too?" I asked. "I can't sing and don't expect I ever will, but I think a man can speak hisself to be heard."

Tom nodded and the truck hit another bump in the road. "And that's a rightful truth too, Blue. Speak well and others will listen."

I thought on that a while and reckoned a man can speak for good or even for hurt, like that Hitler fella overseas. He sure was stirring up trouble again, but I decided not to think on him too much. When I heard him on the radio, he kinda worried me.

***

There was a few scattered farm houses and a small village between Selinsgrove and Sunbury but not much else until you got to the bridge. We rode the remaining half-mile or so without talking. I was thinking about the rest of my journey, and my plan, and home. Tom was humming quietly to himself. His voice was soothing, though not much to think on, but I imagine his picking was a whole might livelier. He had good fingers and I watched him strumming the tunes on his leg.

The Susquehanna ran through the small borough of Shamokan Dam, named for a ten-foot dam destroyed by ice in 1907, or so Tom said. He sure knew a lot for a fella that didn't settle in one place for long. I reckon that went with being a musician. As it turned out, Mr. Willis' recollection of the geography was a might off. The Pennsy—Pennsylvania Railroad—run through Shamokan. This line would take me all the way to Washington, from what Pete had said, and I didn't need to cross the bridge to Sunbury.

"Stop!" I shouted, when I seen the water tank and realized I might not catch the right train if I crossed over.

Even though the truck windows was rolled down against the July heat, the driver didn't hear me.

"I gotta get off here, Tom."

Tom and I both started to thumping the truck bed, and the driver finally heard and slowed down. As soon as he was moving slow enough, I jumped off.

"Nice meeting you, Naples! Good luck with the Woody thing."

"Sure enough, kid, and good luck with whatever you're up to."

I give a salute of gratitude to the driver and his missus. Then run off down a slope toward the water tank. Aware other hobos might be there waiting on the train, I slowed to a walk as I neared it. The grass was high in the field leading to the tank from the west side of the tracks, and a perfect place to shield hobos from police cars cruising the highway. I was right, too. There was at least ten sitting around a small fire, eating what handouts they had got. I had to add the sandwiches that it turned out Mrs. Willis had already placed in my bindle before I even knew it. That explained what she was doing while I was talking to Mr. Willis. She knowed I was leaving. I smiled to myself and said a silent 'thank you.'

"Hey, fellas. Blue's the name."

They welcomed me with a nod and sat along side.

Hobos come and go in the jungles with little regard when it comes to color or creed. A poor man is just as poor if his skin is white or black, if he is a Jew or Christian. It was manmade towns and cities that was segregated. Even I didn't spend much time knowing anyone outside my own kind. I reckon Rudy was the first one, and even then, I didn't spend too much time getting to know him. Believe me, I woulda, but his situation didn't allow.

We was sitting by the fire, in view of the bridge, and passing our foodstuff around along, with a bottle of moonshine. None of the fellas had water and I wasn't taking chances on the river banks in the dark, even with a sliver of moonlight. I took a slug of moonshine and it was all I could do not to spit it out. My throat was on fire. Ain't been much on drinking liquor since.

A couple fellas wandered in on us almost undetected because their skin was too dark for us to see. Once in the firelight I could tell one was a man, I'd say, in his thirties—about my pa's age. The other turned out to be his son, a boy of about ten from the looks of him. They was both wearing torn and patched trousers and shirts. The man's hat was practically in tatters and their shoes was full of holes.

"Been walking a might today," he said. "Thought we could light here for the night."

Nobody said one way or the other, which meant the two was as welcome as I was, so they come in and joined our small circle. By now, it was nearly eleven o'clock but I didn't take out Pete's watch in this company. No telling who you could or could not trust.

The two coloreds pretty much kept silent and listened in on what we was talking about home, why we left, where we was going, and our dreams. Then it come 'round to us waiting for the midnight train, and the colored man started in to singing. I later found out the song was written about the train lights shining in the prison windows down south. They said the train's light was a heavenly light giving the convicts hope. The colored's voice was like an angel and I still hum the song sometimes.

Let the Midnight Special shine a light on me

Let the Midnight Special shine its ever lovin' light on me.

Then come the long low whistle and the train's light shone down the tracks.

"There she is, boys!" one of the'bos shouted and we scurried to pick up our belongings.

Men and boys went to either side of the tracks just a few feet from the water tank. They hunkered down in the brush, waiting to make sure there was no bulls on the tracks.

She slowed to a halt, the brakes squealing at the weight of her. The brakeman and boiler man started filling the tender with water from the tank. I stood in the shadow of the monster engine, so close I could feel her heat—I heard the hiss of her breath. She loomed in the darkness—one hot white eye of a light in the center of her face. Once she had drunk her fill, the brakeman let her go and the train slowly rolled forward, but she picked up speed mighty fast. I looked up as the engine's shadow passed and a sudden dread tied a knot in my belly. I had done this before, but then I had Pete to help and it had been daylight.

Somebody else shouted "Closed cars boys! Up we go!" and I knew my worst fears. We was going to have to run alongside the train, grab for the ladders, and haul ourselves to the top of the cars, then lay flat out and hold on for dear life. I took a deep breath and commenced to running.

Two feet. Three feet. Gotta move faster. My legs was pulling as hard as they could with my shoes pinching on my toes. My head was out in front and my legs was flying off behind. I knew if I misstepped just a little, I'd fall flat and miss the train. If I grabbed hold but lost my footing, I could be pulled clean off and under it. I knew there was boys and men who had their legs torn off or worse.

I pushed hard. The first car passed me by. I pushed harder, and it felt like my lungs was gonna collapse. The second car's ladder was just inches from my fingers—teasing me—begging and spurning me.

"You old hell-train!" I called. "You ain't leaving me behind! You hear?"

With one last lurch, I closed my hands around the ladder. It felt like my arms was pulled from the sockets as I was jerked forward. I kicked up off the ground, and found a rung with my right foot. I pulled the left one up, too and started to climb.

Another tramp had just grabbed on right behind me. If I didn't want him to get yanked clean off the train, I had to climb right fast. I felt the excitement—the blood boiling in my heart—but didn't even have time to let out a shout of elation. I threw myself down on top of the car and hugged her like an old girlfriend—one

I didn't want to let go of. In all, but for the two coloreds who had not planned to be on the train, seven of us made it. We was spread out between three cars. Three of us musta got throwed off or never caught the ladders. Truth is, until the train slowed again and the sun rose, I could have been alone for all I knew. For the next four hours, I pretty much kept my face to the top of the train. When I did turn my head to look across the landscape, all I seen was grey blurs as the Pennsylvania countryside raced past. Every rail set my teeth to rattling. I supposed that was close to hell on earth.

July 5, 1937

The morning sun was bright and hot with no clouds to offer relief. Sitting on the train was about as close to sitting on a stovetop as I could imagine. There was no way anyone could spend the entire day lying face down on that hotbox. As I got no sleep, I felt dizzy when I sat up. Having done this many times before—some for several years—the others was already nibbling on whatever scrap of food they kept back the night before. I hadn't been as wise.

"Hey there, I'm Shorty."

I was somewhat startled by the voice, quavering as it was from the movement of the train. It come from the tramp who had climbed up behind me and had settled next to me for the night. Now by this daylight, I seen he was a boy about my age. He was holding out a biscuit.

"Want some?" he asked.

"Thank you," I replied, breaking off a piece and stuffing it in my mouth without the 'manners of a pig,' as Mama would have said.

"Name's Breadline," I finally managed. And I realized I had not been too friendly just grabbing the food like I did, so I asked, "Where you heading, Shorty?"

"Been asking myself the same question, Breadline. Where am I heading?"

Shorty took his cap, out of his back pocket, give it a slap on his knee, and slid it on his head against the sun. We was both kneeling and I watched as Shorty kind of swayed from side to side with the rhythm of the train. I did too. It was less a sway and more a jerk back and forth.

"Just going where the rails take me." Shorty shifted. "And I guess, going no place fast," he added. "How 'bout you?""Goin' down to D.C." I followed Shorty's lead and placed my cap on my head. "Mighty hot mornin'."

"A might hotter if we was standing still, I suppose."

I laughed. "Yeah, I think you're right."

"You got folks in D.C.?"

By now another hobo, a man of about forty, or at least the creases on his face said so, slid on over to listen in.

"Nope." I answered. "Going to talk to Mrs. Roosevelt about a letter I sent her."

There. I blurted it out, realizing I hadn't really told nobody, not even Pete, my whole reason for travelin'.

"Yeah, I'm going to . . . " I couldn't bring myself to say the rest, to tell them I was planning to ask her for a pot of soup and a dress for my mama. Right then, for the first time, it sounded as ridiculous to me as I suspect it might have sounded to them if I said it out loud.

"How 'bout you, old-timer?" Shorty said, nudging the man with his elbow.

"Willy's the name. Getting off at the next town and going to work for the CCC. I heard they're taking more fellas and it's about time I found some steady work. Who knows, maybe I can find my wife and kids."

I knowed the CCC—the Civilian Conservation Corp—though I reckon Willy was the first person I ever met who was going to join it. It put some thoughts in my head since, I'd be seventeen pretty soon, and they took boys at seventeen. Why, a man working for the CCC not only gets to build things like bridges and parks, camps, roads, and other public works, but he gets meals and money, too. Much of their pay gets sent to family.

I got to wondering how many hobos stopped riding the rails to join up. It was probably the first time I really thought about stories the other tramps might have. Well, there had been Penny and Fred, and their stories was mighty terrible—about abuse and abandon, but here was a man who just wanted to work and find his family again.

I found out that Shorty was a lot like me. He left home because he couldn't stand to hear his pa sobbing at night when his baby sister cried herself to sleep from hunger. Shorty planned to find work and had done some, but as time went by, he just found hisself going on and on, just hoping to be as far from home and all his cares as he could get. Champagne Urbana was his home, over in Illinois.

I whistled. "From what I recall of the maps in school, you're a might far—miles and miles—from home, Shorty. Don't you feel it? Don't you miss it?"

"Not until right now, Breadline. I miss it right now."

He didn't say much more after that. Just sat there with a faraway look in his eyes, and Willy moved back over to wedge hisself for a short snooze against the catwalk running down the center of the car.

I didn't even try to apologize to Shorty for bringing up the memory. I left him on his own, sitting there in his daydream. I guess I thought a boy should think on his home. He sure made me do some of my own, too, especially about the CCC.

***

We rode in silence for a long time, except now we was sitting more comfortable, and the constant rocking of the train coupled with a lack of sleep made my eyes droop.

I suspect we all have those days when we are so tuckered, we fall asleep in any position, any place—heads nodding down, chin to chest or head lolling back, mouth open and drooling on ourselves. Well, it was one of those, only this weren't just falling asleep any ole place. It was falling asleep on top of a fast-moving freight train! It was none too safe and when you wasn't catching bugs between your teeth, you was holdin' on, trying not to get throwed off.

Shorty and me was lucky Willy seen what was happening. I just dozed off and the train come to a curve in the tracks. The empty bindle I carried flew off the train. About the time my chin hit my chest, I was throwed backwards and looking up at the sky. Willy had Shorty by the collar and pulled him to the walkway. Shorty was holding on for dear life.

I was about to roll sidewise and off the train, when out of the blue, another fella who had been walking the top of the car, caught the wind at his back and went flying forward. He caught hisself on the rail and grabbed me with his free hand. After my rude awakening, I had no trouble whatsoever in holding on and pulling myself over to Shorty and Willy, with the other fella crawling behind me.

"You're lucky all you lost is your bindle!" Willy shouted at me. Then he turned to the other fella. "And you! You can't be walking the train like yer strolling down Main Street. You catch a wind on a curve like that . . . Well let's just say, next time you may not be so lucky."

The other fella—a guy in his twenties, I'd say and able to lick Willy if he had a mind—just mumbled some obscenity and let it drop. Besides, his hands was shaking like a leaf and I could tell he had never been so scared in his life.

Once he sat hisself upright again, he said "If I was a cat, I just used up the last of my nine lives. I already used up a few."

We laughed. I guess strain can do that to a man, make him laugh even when he almost died.

It took some time for me to gain my confidence to sit up more and look around. When I did, I seen another three fellas sitting in a gondola car just ahead of us. A small curl of smoke drifted over their heads before disappearing in with the train smoke. They had themselves a cigarette but I never took up the habit and was glad of it. And I was also glad we caught a car so far back from the smoke stack. It was nasty black stuff and I had no leaning to breathe in. Jim—the fella who almost got throwed— and Willy was saying how sometimes the train's smoke gets so bad, especially if you go into a tunnel, you think you might choke to death. Always better to be in the middle of the train.

The train rolled past farmhouses and fields. As we passed one worn out tumble-down shack, a whole family of children come out and waved us on. Me and Shorty waved back. They was smiling like that very moment of seeing us was the best thing in their day, like we was heroes from a Lone Ranger episode disappearing into the sunset. Well, it was actually closer to one in the afternoon, but that's neither here nor there. Then I remembered those long lonesome nights lying awake in my bed listening to the distant train-whistle. It was a sweet and mournful call. I wondered if them kids dreamed of the train like I did.

"Coming to the town fellas," Jim said. "Better get ready to jump off."

"My destination, anyway," said Willy.

"And mine, too," said Shorty.

I looked at him and he beamed.

"Breadline, you and Willy got me to thinking. I been running too long. I turned seventeen last week and I can join the CCC now. I'm going with Willy. Time to start making my way back home."

I felt a strange pain in the pit of my stomach right then. My eyes kinda stung, too. Like maybe I wanted to cry.

The train slowed, and blowed her whistle to let folks at the town-crossing know she was coming in. Jim was already running across the field to the tall grass and Willy was just jumping off.

Shorty turned to me again. "Thank you, Breadline."

"I didn't do nothing. It was you, Shorty. You knew what you had to do."

I was next off, and with my long legs, I was fairly flying across the field to join the other two, but Shorty got his name because of his legs. They was short—there's no nice way to say it—and they was not long enough to make the step down off the ladder to the ground and stay on his feet. One minute he was stepping off into thin air and the next, he was being pulled back toward the train. It was fast, because of the train's speed, and slow because I couldn't fathom what I was seein'.

Someplace in my brain, I knew what was happening and it wasn't good, and yet I couldn't say it or yell it or even move from where I was standing. In fact, I had just come to a stop in my own runnin' and looked back when it happened. Shorty was yanked under the train's wheel onto the track. Shorty's left leg was sucked under the train-wheel onto the track and he tried to throw hisself clear all at the same time. No screams. No blood. Just seconds later, Shorty lying there, not moving.

"Christ," I heard Jim say, and he started to run away from the train. Willy grabbed me by the arm and I was suddenly aware of what had happened, the adrenaline pumping, and we ran back to help Shorty.

Jim shouted back at us. "You better leave him. He's a goner! Nothing you can do, but the bulls will be along."

We ignored his warning and ran. Just ran. Willy threw hisself down next to Shorty and quickly pulled the bandana from his own pocket to tie around Shorty's leg. There was blood after all, and it was everywhere. It was on Shorty's clothes, sprayed across the tracks, smeared in the grass where he apparently had time to drag hisself before losing consciousness, and even in his hair. I wanted to say something but all I could muster was, "Oh God. God. God."

"Lift his head up a bit, Breadline, but not too far. We gotta keep him from going into shock."

I plunked down and lifted Shorty's head into my lap.

"Now, hold this here." Willy had tied his bandana into a tourniquet and made a twist to keep it taunt. I had to hold it so it wouldn't untwist. "I'll go into town for some help."

Shorty's eyes fluttered. He looked up at me and said, "Don't leave me."

I panicked. Alone? I didn't know what to do, if I was left alone. "Willy! Wait!"

He come back and knelt down again. "Stay with us, Willy. I don't want to be alone," I told him quietly so Shorty wouldn't hear. "I don't think help will do."

Shorty's breathing was hard and shallow. There had to be a lot of pain but the shock was so great, he didn't really feel it.

"Got the wind knocked out of me," he gasped.

Even with the tourniquet, the ground was soaking with his blood. Shorty kind of smiled this very strange twisted smile.

"I lost it, didn't I?" He coughed.

"Just rest easy, son," said Willy. "I'm going for help."

"I'm a bleeder," Shorty whispered. "A hemo . . . feel . . . feel . . . "

"Hemophiliac." Willy said.

"Yeah." He coughed some more. Now, Shorty was paler than I ever seen anybody. "Breadline?"

"I'm here." I couldn't see him anymore, not from behind my tears. How could I not cry? I was holding a dying boy in my arms, one like me who only wanted to help his family. He had lost his way, but just now in this town, was going to turn around and go home. Finally go home. He was dying!

Now, I could hear a scuffle, and in the distance near the front of the train I seen bulls.

"We gotta move him," I told Willy. "Please."

As gently as we could, with me on Shorty's right side and Willy on his left, we lifted him and pulled him down the little embankment—the very one which had actually caused his fall. We pulled him into a small gully where we wouldn't be seen. I reckon, looking back now, there was a blood trail, but we didn't think about it. At the time, moving him hadn't been the best plan, but it really didn't matter too much. Shorty only lived long enough to ask me to let his ma know what happened. What else could I do? I said, "I will."

My face was running with tears and snot, and I felt a real solid hot anger inside. It was the bulls' fault! The railroad's fault! They cared so much about a few dollars, they worried about hobos riding the rails and not paying. Was their money so damned important that boys like Shorty, who was scared to be caught, had to die? Like this? In a ditch?

I felt his life leave him as he lie there with his head in my lap and his eyes on me.

Right before he took his last breath, Shorty made me make a promise I couldn't keep. I didn't even know where in Champagne Urbana he lived. Hell, I didn't even know his last name.

"Goddamn you!" I shouted as I leaped to my feet, my fists waving in the air toward the train. "I don't care if you catch me, you damn bulls! Send me to jail, Goddamn it! I don't care anymore!"

Willy grabbed me by the pockets and pulled me down.

"Shut up, boy. Get a grip on yourself."

I turned on Willy and woulda pounded the living daylights out of him, but he said something that brung me back to my senses.

"If we leave him here, they will follow the blood and give him a burial. Come on, son, you need to get to Washington."

He was right. Willy needed to find his family and I needed to get back to mine. The best we could do for Shorty was play it out the way we planned.

"I gotta know something, Willy. How'd you know what to do? I mean, how to take care of him, the bleeding and all?"

Willy was silent a moment, then he replied. "Before this all started—this Depression—I was going to school to be a doctor, Breadline. I almost made it. Just one more year to go, but we couldn't find the money to pay. I had a wife, and a second kid on the way."

"You went to school pretty old," I said before I realized it was probably rude.

Only, Willy laughed. "I look a might older than I am. Life can do that to a man. Now, we better get going or we'll be found out for sure."

We hopped up to run and the bulls give chase.

Trouble Follows

It really didn't take long to lose the railroad police. They was not interested in chasing two bums across fields and through brambles. Once we stopped running, I commenced to shaking all over. The truth took hold—I just held another boy my age as he died in my arms.

"Jesus," I heard myself swear, and Mama reached out from my head and slapped me across the mouth.

"Don't you ever let me hear you use the Lord's name unless it's in prayer, William Saxton, nor any other cuss words neither, or you'll taste soap for a week. You hear me?"

"But Mama, his blood is on my overalls. That poor boy's blood. Mama, I can't keep my word and tell his folks. What am I gonna do?"

Only Mama weren't there to answer or advise. Only Willy was there.

"Son, you all right?"

I come 'round to my senses at the sound of his voice.

"I expect," I replied, though in truth I weren't too sure.

"You can double back and catch the train out, or you're welcome to come with me into Reading. It's a fair-size city and you can pick up some handouts. 'Course, I'm shipping on out with the next men for the Conservation Corp. How old are you?"

"Sixteen. I don't turn seventeen until July 13. 'Sides, I gotta get to Washington."

"Suit yourself. Just don't wait too long to get the train. Stay on the farside of the train away from the tank so nobody sees you." Willy took two steps then turned back and threw out his hand. "And good luck, kid. I am really sorry about what happened to your friend."

***

I waited a tick or few after Willy left, then I walked to the train thinking about what Willy said about staying out of sight, and about Shorty being my friend. Was Shorty my friend? Can you know somebody for so little a time and have them be like folks you knowed a might longer? Like Penny and Fred? Even they weren't so close. Yet I had to wonder if it made any sense not to call them friends. Maybe friendship is about shared experiences, shared laughs, and shared troubles. Lord knows Penny, Fred, Shorty, and me all had those. So, yeah. Shorty was my friend and I had to make sure he was okay.

After seeing the bulls was gone, I made my way back to the little gully upwind of the train. You couldn't miss the smear of blood reaching from the tracks down the embankment, and sure enough, just like Willy said, Shorty was gone. There was plenty of footprints around so I suspect the police took him off and I was satisfied. The idea he might lie there alone until his bones was picked clean by critters was horrible to me. At least I hoped he would be given a good burial. And I made one of the hardest promises to myself that I ever made—I would find Shorty's ma, just like I said. I didn't know how, but I was gonna do it.

***

The old devil train let out a whistle and begun pulling out. I seen a pack of tramps rise up from the brush and run for the train and so did I—this time without a bindle, as mine had blown from the train—and more sure-footed, not wanting Shorty's fate to be my own. As luck would have it, I found an open car this time and threw myself up. The fellas there before me grabbed my arms and pulled me in. I only wish I knew what our "Next Town" would be and how far from D.C. we was.

I reckon I'm not sure why fellas think riding the rails is an adventure. Seeing different places and meeting folks—sure—but days and nights on the train with nothing much to do can only get a fella into trouble. Maybe that's why there are so many bums folks would just rather be rid of. Then there are folks like Pete, Fred and Penny, good folks just down on their luck.

I didn't have too much to say. I was still thinking about Shorty. I just sat with my back up against the boxcar wall and some crates being hauled. I sat there wedged in somewhat of a corner and looked over the other fellas. There was four of them—a couple growed men, and a couple boys maybe age ten and eleven. The men? I'd say was in their twenties, but with all the dirt ground into our faces, it gets right hard to judge. I listened in over the clickity-clack of the rails beneath the train wheels. Rocking from side to side with the rhythm, their words was sing-song.

"I knowed this one broad up New York way would make your mouth water. What a pistol."

"Got no use for dames. I always hated my sisters."

"Anybody got a Camel?"

"Nope, smoked my last butt waiting for the train."

"What's he lookin' at?'

"You a pansy?"

"Hey, kid, he's talkin' to ya. You a pansy?"

It took me a minute to realize he was talking to me.

One of the older fellas, wearing Levis and a torn, stained undershirt, stood up and wove his way across the car to stand in front of me. He kicked my foot and in a loud voice asked again, speaking each word like I was deaf, "ARE YOU A GOD DAMN PANSY, BOY?"

"Go to H . . . ," My words trailed off before I got slapped by Mama again. "No. I'm just tired."

He turned back toward the others and mocked, “Says he’s just tired.”

“Hey, he’s got blood on his pant leg,” the youngest boy said, standing to walk over. “You bleeding?”

“Back off, Buddy,” the thug said. I can’t think of a more polite word for him than ‘thug.’

“No, kid, I ain’t hurt,” I called past him. “Thanks for askin’.” Then to the thug I said, “Look I don’t want no trouble here. I just want to ride the train and mind my own business. It ain’t been a good day.”

“Hey, Brady,” the other twenty-year-old called. “Leave him alone will ya? Look I found a butt. You can have it. It’ll take the edge off.”

Brady kicked my foot again for good measure, like a dog lifting his leg on a tree, and went back to join his friends. Obviously, the four of them had been traveling together awhile. I just didn’t want to get in on any new friendships right now. By the looks of Brady and the other fella, who I found out was called Hooligan, I reckon it was best.

From my seat, I could see through the open boxcar door as the landscape passed by—trees, one, two, three, four, five and more trees—a farm house, a field, a coal mine, a steel mill, trees, one, two, three . . . I surely missed seeing the river. No way of telling what the other side of the landscape looked like, but I reckon there was fields and farms, and coal mines too. This was big mining country, so the fields that wasn’t being farmed was pretty torn up with mining equipment. Absentmindedly, I picked at the blood on my pant leg. Guess I hoped to rub it off, but there was always going to be a shadow there. I imagine that’s not all bad really. Thinking on such a tragedy, how could anyone forget? As for remembering, well Mama always said those memories, sorrowful though they might be, went into the pockets of what made people who they was. She said if ever they found themselves forgetting, they should reach in and take it out. Yessir. I got Shorty’s blood in my pocket, and a mind to give the railroad a share of it someday.

***

Hard to say how much time passed. Pete's watch remained safely tucked in my overalls, but the shadows was leaning. It had been after two when the train pulled out of Reading. I musta dozed a tick because I was startled awake by Brady's voice and the sound of bones knocking against each other as Hooligan sent a pair of dice down to the far wall of the car..

"Come on, seven! Seven, come eleven!"

"Acey, Deucey. You losey," said the boy they called Buddy.

I sat up from where I had slid over with my head on a crate and rubbed my stiff neck.

"Hey, kid." I said the older of the two boys. "I'm Blue." He was standing back and not playing the game. "Don't you craps?"

"No. I got no money to lose." He nodded toward the game. "You?"

"No. What's your name?"

"Little Joe, cuz my uncle is big Joe," he replied, sitting next to me.

"Winner!" Brady called. He looked at Buddy as he scooped up his winnings. "Too bad, kid."

"Yeah, too bad," said Hooligan, counting out a few dollar bills.

I got to wondering where the boys got so much cash when I reached in my overalls' pocket to make sure Pete's watch and what I made from Mr. Willis was still there. It was. Little Joe didn't seem to notice. He was busy calling his brother to come sit.

"Don't mind them, Bud. I didn't play and we can still get something to eat in Philly."

"Is Philly the next stop?" I asked.

"Yessir," said Joe, "and end of the line for us. We're going home. Got tired of this traveling around." He slapped his knee and a little cloud of dust rose. "Always dirty. Always hungry. What I wouldn't give for some clean clothes. Not what we thought it would be."

"Yeah," added Buddy, looking over at the two men picking up their dice and winnings. "Not worth the troubles."

"Amen to that," I added. In a low voice I asked, "They give you much trouble?"

"Well," said Joe. "you seen 'em and how they tried to get you into a fight and how they won the craps. They cheat and anything else they can so's to get what they want."

Hooligan glanced over and Joe shut up, hoping he hadn't been overheard.

"I see Pansy Boy is talking. He propositioning you, little men?"

Joe and Buddy was about to speak out but I stood up instead.

"Look, I got no beef with you two. I just want to be left alone."

"Yeah?" said Brady, walking over and sticking his nose in my face. "Well, I reckon we got no beef to give ya, Pansy Boy. And you neither," he said spitting on Buddy's shoe.

"Why, you dirty . . . "

Joe's words faded as the two men drew closer to him. I stuck my arm out. "Leave the kids alone."

"Or what?"

"Or you and I will have a talk at the next stop, or what. I ain't no pansy. Told you before. Even if I was, I could lick you, and I ain't afraid of you."

I felt my jaw tighten and my finger dig into my palms as I balled my fists just in case. Brady poked a boney finger in my chest and shoved. "Next stop, hard ass."

From then on, one or the other of us three stayed awake and there was an invisible line drawn across the boxcar. Hooligan and Brady constantly took turns grimacing at whoever was on watch. Now and then, they stood or stomped heavy to scare us. One time during the night, Brady stood to piss off the train and made sure he sprayed Buddy as he turned back from the door. The kid was asleep so I just wiped him off and let him sleep on. I never told him what happened. Those two thugs was adding up counts on my mental list.

It was Little Joe's early morning watch when the train give a sudden jerk, then stopped and woke all of us at once.

"What the . . . ?" Brady was first to the door. "Can't tell. Too far up the tracks and still kinda dark."

He hopped down and Hooligan followed.

"Stay here," I told the two boys. "I'll have a look see."

As I walked down the side of the train, careful not to be seen by any officials, several faces peered out of open cars and down from the top of the train. "What's up, Mack?" they asked.

I know it's just an expression, but being called Mack after meeting a real one in Selinsgrove didn't sit well. Yet, I knew they meant nothing on it.

"Can't tell just yet. Sit tight."

My path was blocked by Brady and Hooligan and a couple other tramps who was curious. They wasn't letting me pass.

"Look, now is not the time to fight. What's up?"

One of the other tramps, who didn't know about our beef, spat the answer. "Something on the rails, maybe a tree. They're working on it."

I reckon I didn't feel comfortable standing out in the open. Besides, I seen plenty a fallen tree in the woods by the house and others up at Pa's mill. If the others wanted to chance being spotted, it was their business. I walked back to the car, passing the word along as I went, "Just a fallen tree."

The boys wasn't no place to be seen when I got back to the car."Fellas, where are you?"

They poked their heads out from behind the stacked crates. "We're here. Too close to home to get caught now, Blue."

"How'd you like to ride the rest of the way in peace? Without those other two glaring at ya?"

"Reckon we'd like that, all right."

"Okay then, get me that board over there."

I had intended to find a way to wedge the boxcar door closed with us inside but the sliders was outside and so was the handle. I felt a might foolish and could have kicked myself for not noticing before.

"Come on, we'll switch cars. At least we won't have to ride with 'em."

After checking to be sure the thugs wasn't in sight, we three headed on back several cars to another open car with nobody in it.

"Reckon this one will do."

"Thanks, Blue," Buddy said. "When we make Philly, you gotta come to our place."

"I think your folks will want some time alone with you. How long you been gone?"

"Oh, not too sure," said Buddy looking at his brother. "Maybe a week or two. Maybe three?"

Joe added, "We just wanted something to do."

"I see," I said.

I couldn't muster much more as I thought about two boys off on an adventure where folks got killed. Their mama musta been worried sick.

"Really, Blue, come meet our folks."

"I'll think on it."

We climbed onboard and settled in just as the train whistle blew. It let the crew know they was getting underway. Looking back out the door, I could just make out the shadows of Brady and Hooligan entering our old car. The train lurched forward so there was no chance of them coming to look for us. Daylight was beginning to spread over the countryside and the three of us caught some extra peaceful sleep, only waking when we heard the familiar squeal of the brakes.

"Philly!"

"Home!"

"One more stop."

July 6, 1937
Greenwich Freight Yard

We was riding the "Pennsy Line" and Philadelphia was her home. In fact, I found out from Buddy and Joe, it was money from Philly that built the Pennsylvania Railroad. It was a piece of ironic that this very train was coming home with the boys. But me? I was still a day from my destination and miles from my home. But, I did feel their excitement and reveled in it.

It was a grey, dingy, drizzling, mid-morning by the time the train pulled into the yard. There was a cool breeze and so we was as bundled up as we could be. I wore both Pete's shirt and my cap and still felt the cold.

We didn't jump off the train until it slowed to almost a crawl. As long as there weren't no freight men in view, the boys and me had some time to gaze out over the sea of tracks and trains. I don't reckon I'd ever seen nothin' so immense before, just one track after the other. They was lined up like I imagined all them roads leading to Rome in the history book at school. Why there musta been ten to fifteen tracks coming in with almost as many trains loading and unloading. It was hard to make out the buildings beyond them trains but I could see the tops of the three story brick warehouses, and some a water tanks and machinery for unloading heavier cargo. There was some movin' belts for taking goods into the warehouses and of course equipment for unloading the gondolas. I had to wonder how anyone knew which train went where and I even begun to worry how I was gonna figure out which one rode to Washington.

"Come on, Blue!" Joe shouted as he leaped down to the ground. Buddy threw him his bindle and nearly jumped into his brother's arms. He was so excited. I followed.

Before we crossed the first track, Joe held out his arm to keep us back until he looked long down the line. It was almost the only track with no cars on it, and once he was sure no train was pulling in, he lowered his arm and we crossed. Seemed they'd done this a time or two before and was cautious enough.

Hopping over rails and weaving among the cars and between the fat raindrops, I followed the two brothers over several tracks until we stood beneath a water tank and ducked down a narrow corridor between two brick buildings. The space was fenced off but there was a hole and we squeezed through it, out into an alley. I never did give Brady or Hooligan another thought after we switched cars, but they sure enough thought of me, because they was—waiting on the outside of the yards. Brady was holding a piece of old two-by-four he picked up along the way.

"Well, well. Looks like the pansy boy forgot his promise," Brady said, slapping the board on his palm. "You forget you was gonna lick me, Pansy Boy?"

"Come on, Blue," said Joe. "Don't pay them no mind."

"Yeah Blue," said Buddy, tugging insistently on my sleeve, which, by now, was plastered to my body from the rain. We all looked a might liked drowned rats.

"Sure, Pansy Boy. Go with your little friends."

By this time I had enough and turned toward Brady, pushing the boys off to one side.

"Look, I told you twice before. I ain't no pansy, but I guess you must be deaf. I don't want no fight with you and your pal there." I nodded toward Hooligan. "But then, you don't seem to have no sense. So, if you want a fight, you got it."

While I was talking, I was rolling up my sleeves and tossed my cap to Buddy.

"Now, which one of you is gonna be first?" I asked. "And, I reckon, if you ain't no cowards, you'll put that board up and fight like real men."

Brady give me a twisted smirk and dropped the board with a heavy thud.

"Reckon it's gonna be me who teaches you the lesson, boy."

I made note—he left off the name-calling, this time—he was going to be more bluster than bust. I stood with my legs slightly apart for balance, fists balled, arms bent at the elbow like I figured the boxers might stand waiting in the ring.

Brady laughed and doubled over. "What the hell you doing? You got somethin' in your pants, boy?" He spat on the ground.

It was more than obvious to me, he wanted me to make the first move but I just stood my ground—firm in my stance—waiting for him.

"Come on, Brady. Let's get this over with," Hooligan said.

"Don't rush me," Brady replied.

"Well?" I asked.

"Ya comin' or not?" Hooligan said impatiently.

Brady took a step toward me and grit his teeth at me. "Ah hell, you ain't worth tearin' up the skin on my knuckles."

He jumped toward the boys and they backed with a startle.

"You and your little friends," he spat again. "Come on, Hooli, I'm getting soaked."

The two of them turned and walked back toward the yards as quickly as they had appeared. Buddy picked up the board and hauled it after them.

"Run away, sissies!" he shouted.

"Let 'em run, Buddy," said Joe. "You was pretty brave, Blue."

"I reckon I know their kind by now—all talk and no action. Still, it could have gone either way. Brady was right about one thing."

"What's that?"

"We're gettin' soaked. Let's get out of this wet."

***

Joe and Buddy knew this neighborhood so I reckoned they didn't live too far off, but it was raining harder and instead of heading on home, we took shelter in an abandoned building just east of the yard, in a small industrial property. Most of the windows had been broken out. Looking around, we found enough dry debris, and with the one last match Joe had in his pocket, we built us a fire to take off the chill. Mid-morning or not, it felt more like early evening. It was so gloomy.

While we was standing with our hands held out over the fire and little waves of steam rising off our wet clothes, I happened to look out past Joe's head through one of the broken glass window shards. I spied a patch of blue grey—not sky, but water.

"What's the water over yonder?"

"Oh yeah, well you wouldn't know, would ya? That's the Delaware River," Joe replied.

I took off my cap and give it a slap to get the rain out.

"You mean the river George Washington crossed? I'll be danged," I said.

Moving over to the window, I pretended I could see the river clear as day beyond buildings and trees, and the sheet of rain pouring from the roof.

"I never expected to see something from the history books, but then again, I am goin' to the Capitol, ain't I? Imagine that."

"Sure 'nuff, it is the very one, Blue. Philly is full of history when ya got time and money to have a look-see." He poked his brother in the arm. "Hey, Buddy, you remember the Museum of Art? The teacher took us to see it just before Ma and Pa lost the house."

"I sure do, and them men what was living under the walls?" Buddy said excitedly. "Blue, these Bos was so needy, they dug in under a wall for shorin' up an embankment next to the museum. Well, really they was livin' in the sewer down there. We found it when the teacher weren't lookin'. Only, she wouldn't let us go in explorin'."

"Oh yeah, I forgot," said Joe to Buddy. "Kinda funny now, don't you think?" Joe turned back to me. "See, Blue, Pa had a good job working in the factory and Ma stayed home. There's three more of us for her to look after. But when the factory closed down, this very factory we're in as a matter of fact . . . "

"Your pa worked here?"

"Sure did," said Buddy. "They made dishes here for restaurants all over the country."

That explained it then. I seen bits of broken pottery on the floor, and an overhead conveyer, I reckon woulda been leading to the kilns.

"Well, Pa couldn't pay the mortgage and the bank foreclosed on the house. I'm almost embarrassed to tell ya where we live now, being we invited you to come meet our folks and all."

"It's okay. I seen bad, and I reckon your mama keeps it as well as she can. No need to feel sick on it, unless you don't want me to come after all."

"Oh no, we want you to come," said Buddy. "Only, there won't be no place for you to stay proper, and maybe not us neither."

"What he's trying to say, Blue, is we live in a shantytown. Heck, we only been gone a short while and, even then, no telling what it will be like. People come and go, and well, the shanties don't always hold up to weather like this."

"How far is your home?" I asked. I deliberately used the word 'home' because I think there's nothin' sadder than a person feeling life let 'em down and they got no place to call their own. Mama always said a man could live in a house, but his home was something he made in his heart. It went beyond walls, a floor and a roof. These poor boys . . .

Buddy suddenly shouted. "The rain stopped! Let's get goin', Joe!"

Joe was already snuffing out the fire by kicking dirt over it, and Buddy was standing in the street. We started walking right away, and I was feeling warmer and dryer already. The sun come out to help dry up what the fire didn't get. After a heavy downpour on a July day, a mugginess settles in the air. Being in the city, I reckon the air was a might closer all the time.

We walked west past the train yard and I took careful note in my head of the street names. Tasker to Greenwich, then south along Front, ten or twenty blocks to Oregon, and then west to 3rd and 4th Streets. All total, it took us about twenty minutes to walk to the edge of the shantytown. The closer we got, the lighter the boys' steps appeared and the more folks seemed to know them. Yep, this was their neighborhood.

Giuseppe's Ristorante

Factory lots melted into row houses and tenements. We passed newsies selling the latest edition, and it all blended into streets with grocers, fruit stands, slow-moving automobiles and delivery trucks. We smelled food from local eateries and heard babies crying. Everywhere, people walked across streets, talking loudly. Dogs barked. The sights and sounds were a far cry from Wellsboro or Selinsgrove.

Buddy disappeared up three concrete steps into a shop. The sign over the door read *Giuseppe's Ristorante.* I just stood there pondering the sign.

Buddy popped his head out from the doorway and waved us in. "Come on!"

"It says 'Giuseppe.' It means 'Joseph' in Italian," said Joe. "This is my Uncle Joe's restaurant. We won't be long."

I offered to wait outside but Little Joe grabbed my arm.

"Trust me, you want to come in."

Like Willis' General Store, the café had that wood-floor smell I like so much, but it was mixed with the smell of tomato sauce, rich spices, and fresh baked bread. For the first time in a day or two, I realized my hunger. I hadn't had anything to eat since Reading.

"Oh, my boys!" called a round man with a balding head. His nose was bulbous and a thick mustache shaded his mouth. The apron he wore, once white I'm sure,was splattered with sauce and stained with charcoal. "Come on in and have a seat. Where on earth you been? Everyone been so worried."

Joe and Buddy walked toward a booth near the back.

"But first, how about a hug for your old zio?"

The boys went to his arms readily and received the biggest hug I'd ever seen, but then, Uncle Joe was a big man. It's a wonder they weren't covered in sauce, too.

"And who we got here?" he said, looking at me.

"Zio, this is Blue."

"I should say so," Uncle Joe blurted. "Just look at them eyes. Hey, Mama! Come here and look at this boy's eyes. They's as blue as the heavens!"

A woman come through the kitchen doorway. She was almost as round as her husband, and big-bosomed. Her dark hair was tucked into a neat bun on the back of her head with wisps of hair stuck out the sides around her ears. It truthfully made her look like an exotic animal, but her smiling eyes and curled full lips said *woman.*

"Oh, my goodness! Papa, you're right!" She walked up to me and, without so much as a 'how do you do,' stuck her hands on both sides of my face and give me a big wet kiss on the forehead.

"Hey, Zia, you kissing the strangers before you kiss your own nephews?" asked Little Joe.

Aunt Rosie swung around. "Bambinos! Mi Amours." She swept them up into her large arms and pressed their faces to her bosom. I thought they might suffocate. Then, just as quickly she pushed them away.

"Papa, whatsa matter with you? These boys look half-starved. Why aren't they sitting and eating? Fool of a man." She frowned at her husband but turned to the boys with a smile. "Sit, Bambinos and you, too, blue eyes."

"His name's Blue, Zia," said Buddy.

"Of course it is!" Aunt Rosie waved her arms in the air and raced back to the kitchen. "Coming up, boys!" she called over her shoulder.

Uncle Joe shrugged. "Like I said, boys, have a seat." Then to me, with an elbow nudge to my arm, "My Rosie is quite a woman, Blue. You should be so lucky."

Joe and Buddy slid into the booth and I took the bench across from them.

After the flurry of greetings, I finally had the chance to notice the cafe and the other patrons. There was red and white checkered tablecloths and the whole place was warm and cozy. There was other tables and booths in the café but they was empty. When I asked Buddy why, he said because it weren't suppertime yet.

"It'll fill up," he added.

The patrons was all men in work-a-day clothes and it was obvious they was on their way home from a hard day's labor. They sat at the bar with their beers—their trousers and short sleeves soiled with sweat and grease. You could even see the grease under their stubby fingernails. They was all smiling at the little display of affection Rosie had shown her nephews.

"Hey, Giuseppe," said one. "You don't suppose I could pretend to be a long lost relative? Your Rosie gives good bear-hugs!"

Uncle Joe was as good-natured a man as I ever seen. He just flicked his hand at the fella, obviously a neighborhood regular, and said, "You should be so lucky."

In a matter of minutes, Aunt Rosie appeared again from the kitchen with a huge platter overflowing with spaghetti and meatballs. Uncle Joe helped set the table with three clean white plates, knives, forks, spoons, matching checkered napkins, and a basket of bread. Just as fast as they placed it in front of us, we tucked the napkins under our chins. We was bibbed and eating.

Uncle Joe went to the bar and Aunt Rosie stood nearby with her arms on her hips, watching us.

"Slow down, Bambinos. You got all the time you want."

The boys apologized to her for eating so fast and I made sure to thank her for the kindness. She smiled her beautiful wide smile again.

"You are welcome, Blue. Any friend of the boys is a friend of ours. Now mange! Eat."

Uncle Joe come back from the bar with a bottle that looked like it was wrapped in a basket, and five glasses.

"Chianti!" Giuseppe announced.

He poured some of the dark red wine into each glass then held his out.

"A toast to our returning bambinos. May their mama be at peace with their return . . . and to our friend, Blue. Salute!"

I watched as the four of them drained their glasses in almost one gulp—which wasn't too difficult because they weren't full—and I did the same. My first wine weren't half bad—better than moonshine anyway.

"Now, you eat up, boys while I go let your mama know you're home."

When he said that, Little Joe grabbed his shirt-sleeve.

"Zio, was she very worried?"

"Well, what do you think, Joey? Her boys disappeared without a trace, and no word for almost three weeks."

Joe and Buddy both hung their heads.

"Yeah, we shouldn't have done that, Zio, but let us surprise her. Please?"

Uncle Joe grunted, and for the first time since we arrived, I sensed he might have been disappointed in the boys.

"Well, as long as you go home when you are finished here and take something to the family when you go."

"We will, Zio!"

Now I never had spaghetti or meatballs as good as those before, and it had been a very long time since I ate anything meaty. I reckon I ate too much all at once because my stomach felt a might queasy. I also ain't drunk wine before, neither, but the boys reassured me it was the norm and it would help digest the sauce.

Aunt Rosie packed a large basket with food for us to take to the boys' mama and give them one more bear hug. Uncle Joe had a handshake for each of us. I did not escape Aunt Rosie's bosom, I might add. Just two steps toward the door and she grabbed me and pulled me in for the hug. Aunt Rosie smelled like herbs and bread, and I never forgot that scent. Since then, whenever I am around fresh-baked bread, her bosom is the first thing to flash before my eyes—then those smiling eyes and curled full lips. While it is most strange and comical, I reckon, memories of Rosie are a great comfort.

One Too Many Hoovervilles

We left Giuseppe's with the boys carrying the basket between them. We only walked another block, just past 3rd Street, when the Hooverville come into view. I wasn't expecting what we seen. The shacks was all built up willy-nilly in a vacant lot taking up an entire city block on Oregon Avenue between Third and Fourth Streets. It stretched out—a field full of cardboard, scrap metal, old tires, and whatever a man could find to use as building materials—here and there a chimney pipe in the "wealthier" shanties. No telling how many people was living there. The heavy rain from morning had turned the lot into a quagmire, and everything in it was splattered with muddy earth nearly head to toe—people, dogs, and a bicycle or two. The boys stopped at the edge of the makeshift village. They sure looked confused, like they been gone for years.

"Don't you know which one is yours?" I asked. I reckon I could see why. They pretty near looked the same, and in this muddy mess, I'd have trouble too.

"Oh, it's not that so much, Blue," Little Joe said. "It's just . . . well, we're happy to be home."

What an odd thing, I thought. How could they be happy to be home in that place? Just look at what they called home. I was befuddled, and I admit, a bit teary-eyed. I never lived in a shack except for the incident with Mack. Ma and our grassy yard seemed so far away. I'd been homesick for a spell and now this just made it worse.

"Well don't you reckon you oughta get a move on then? Your folks will be glad to see you."

"In this mud, nobody's going very far very fast, Blue. Trust us on this one. We'll walk up a block and double back. Our place is on the other side anyway."

We walked back a few steps and headed on up Third to Shunk Street. The shantytown was on our left just beyond a tangle of brush all the way around the block. As we moved, I gazed over the invisible wall dividing the world I knew from this strange way of life—a wall dividing the haves and have-nots. Strange as that sounds, right then, I felt like a have.

This was real poverty and yet the folks I seen was everyday folks, outside cleaning up after the storm—trying to make the most of what they had. Why, more than one shack had a tiny garden with vegetables growing—though soggy after the storm. And one was even more like a small fishing cottage with straight wood planks and a platform porch on stilts hanging over a drop in the landscape! A rocking chair sat empty on that porch. All around, I seen wash tubs with washboards for laundry, wooden and tin buckets for fetching water, a few stumps of old trees, fire pits, shovels, axes—all the things one would expect to see at a country home like, well, like my folks'. Only, this was in the middle of a big city—a city that helped found a nation. And these folks was factory workers and such, not farmers. It was almost more than I could take in at once. The images of children playing, dogs barking, and coffee pots over open wood fires in the middle of Philadelphia was something to remember.

We almost traversed the entire block when, finally, we come to a funny little gate. It seemed so odd seeing it because these was shacks and there was no privacy—no property rights. They was squatters, could be kicked off by whoever owned the lot, which was most likely the city.

The gate was made of wood pickets and suspended on two hinged posts placed tight between two shacks, so you had to open it to get to the shack right behind it. I reckon the boys seen me looking quizzical.

"The gate was Mama's idea," said Buddy. "She said if she was gonna raise her family in an open field in the city, she was gonna have some civilized ways—no wild-Indian children running amok. She wanted a gate like the one we had at our real house."

Just then, we was interrupted by a woman's excited voice, followed by that of what I reckoned was the boys' younger brother and sisters.

"Buddy! Joseph!"

"Mama!" The two threw open the gate and rushed to the waiting woman's arms.

"Oh, my dear boys!"

I stepped back so as to let them have their private family moment and wondered if my ma would give me such a welcome, or whether she'd be angry and ready with the strap. In fact, the thought hit me—I didn't even know if my pa was still alive. I reckon it was the first time I thought on it since I left home almost a month ago. I thought about turning back, but Washington was just a day away. By tomorrow, I could be sitting in the White House waiting to talk to the First Lady herself.

"Come here, son."

The boys' mama was speaking to me. I took off my cap and held it in front of me with the respect my folks taught me I oughta.

"Yes, Ma'am."

"My sons tell me you kept them safe. Is that right? I'm mighty grateful to you."

"Well, Ma'am, I really can't take no credit. I only met them . . . " I was going to say I only met them a day or two ago but she interrupted me.

"Well, no matter, son, you were with them and that's all I need to know. You come on in."

Until then, I was standing outside the gate waiting for an invite.

"Thank you kindly, Ma'am."

"Oh none of that 'ma'am' stuff. 'Round here, everybody calls me Mama Lee, and I reckon you can call me Mama Lee too, if you like."

"Thank you, Ma'am, er, Mama Lee."

The boys was already off taking the basket of food from the café into their tiny shack. Seeing it from the front, their shanty couldn'ta been big enough for such a large family. Once Mama Lee led me inside, I found I was right. It was nothing but one large room with some pallets from a factory. Mr. Lee made them into two beds in one corner, and there was an old handmade quilt serving as a divider for Mr. and Mrs. Lee's privacy. Behind the quilt was their old four-poster bed with the posts sawn down to fit under the low roof. There was a wood-burning stove that Mrs. Lee said her husband had been able to salvage it from the plate factory office. He had rigged up the smokestack to go through the corrugated tin roof. There was four chairs and a table they had managed to bring from their old house. Plates, bowls, saucers and cups—all factory seconds—was stacked on a wide board serving as a shelf over a washtub the family used for cleaning.

Seeing how they had to live made me remember what my school teacher told us about the homes of the early settlers and how they used what she called a 'sideboard'. It was just an old board which could be placed on top something when eating, then either taken down for more room, or used as a bed. Unlike a pioneer sideboard, the Lees' table took up most of the extra space but it was a might more comfortable, I reckon. I'm sure it made Mrs. Lee feel more civilized. I realized these folks was like the early pioneers in a way, and I knew they musta had stamina and courage or they woulda dried up and died.

In one corner there was a bucket, filled with water that still dripped off from the ceiling after the morning rain. Another bucket served as a toilet to be emptied into a pit shared by several families, so Buddy said. Except for rainwater, I can't imagine where they got their clean drinking water, and I felt it might be rude to ask. I suppose they might have sent the children to the river or to Giuseppe's, or maybe even another nearby business. The floor was just more salvaged material—some loose boards laid down on the dirt. A couple mismatched pieces of old linoleum covered most of it.

"I'm sorry Mr. Lee isn't here to greet you, Blue. That is your name, right?"

"Yes, Ma'am. I mean, Mama Lee. Most folks call me Blue."

"Well, Blue, Mr. Lee is off looking for a piece of roof to patch that spot. It tore open during the hard downpour. I'm surprised you boys weren't drenched to the skin."

"We was, but Buddy and Joe made a fire."

"Good. I'm glad my boys know how to fend for themselves. It's about the only way we can live, these days."

Buddy and Joe had placed the basket of food on the table, saying it was from their zio and zia. Two ticks later, the boys scurried off at the insistence of their younger siblings, to go help their Pa find what he needed to repair the roof.

"They are good boys, Blue. We're more than blessed by their Godparents Joseph and Rosie. Did you meet them?"

"Yes, Ma'am, and they was right nice. Fed us and all."

"Yes, Rosie is the best cook in Philadelphia, in my opinion. If it weren't for this damned Depression, she'd have a big fancy place the way she always dreamed, over on East Passyunk Avenue. I hope she gets her dream someday, Blue."

"Ma'am . . . Mrs. Lee . . . I hope you don't mind me prying, but I was wondering—Giuseppe and his wife, they're Italian . . . and . . ."

"And, how can they be the boys' aunt and uncle?"

"Yes, Ma'am."

"Blue, when my children was born they was born into the Catholic Church, and they each got a Godparent to help raise them. Their pa was a regular at Giuseppe's—their eventual Godfather's place. My husband Ford, the boys' pa, loves to tell jokes. He and Joseph used to banter back and forth until the two of them was bent over from laughter. They couldn't help but become fast friends."

Mama Lee picked up a broom and swept some dust out the door.

"When my first two was born, we asked Joseph and Rosie Torantini to become part of our family. Things was so different back then, Blue, back when we was able to give the Torantinis a leg up. Now it's them helping us. That's a real friendship."

I just caught Mrs. Lee wiping a tear from her eye when Mr. Lee appeared in the doorway.

"Emma, come see what I found!"

Mama Lee held her hand over her heart, startled by his sudden appearance and excited announcement.

Both the Lee parents was on the tall and leanish side. Mr. Lee stood above his wife by only an inch or two—not like my folks where Pa stood at least six inches taller than Mama. Mr. Lee's smile lit the darkened shack and his excitement was infectious.

"Ford, we have company. This is Blue."

"Oh howdy, Blue. The boys told me all about you. Fine lad!" Mr. Lee wasted no time getting back to his wife. "Now, Emma, you come take a look at your new roof tile so I can get it up before dark."

"Excuse, me Blue, my husband is like a kid when he finds something new. We better go see or he'll be like a puppy—yappin' until we do."

Me and Mama Lee went outside to join the rest of the family and a gathering of shanty neighbors. Mr. Lee stood holding a piece of tin about two-foot by a foot and a half. He turned it backwards so his wife couldn't see the front, but it was embossed so you could tell it was a sign.

"Now, Emma, close them brown eyes."

She sighed with frustration at his childlike insistence but did as he asked. Mr. Lee turned the tin around.

"Ta dah!" the boys shouted.

"Okay, little woman," said Mr. Lee, "take a gander at your new roof!"

The expression on Mrs. Lee's face was a mixture of quizzicalness, embarrassment, and joy all at once. There, staring back at her in bold black and gold, was a sign:

BE KIND TO THE HORSE
USE CAVANAUGH'S
WONDER COLIC REMEDY
SAFETY FIRST IN ALL CASES OF COLIC
ASK YOUR DRUGGIST FOR CAVANAUGH'S

Then there was the company name and logo, and some other writing in small letters.

I knowed how my mama woulda reacted and I suspect I knew what was going through Mama Lee's mind, but she smiled and said, "Why, Ford, it's remarkable," then she added "Don't miss dinner. Rosie sent a basket."

I said I would stay outside a spell and watch as Mr. Lee placed his new sign. The only saving grace, was it wasn't going to patch a wall where everybody would see it, so much as the roof where the slight pitch would hide it somewhat. Buddy and Joe was blushing as some of the neighbors laughed at the whole scene, and I smiled.

"Why doesn't he just face it around so the back of the sign is out?" I whispered to Little Joe.

"Because, then it wouldn't be no fun." He replied.

It was nothing if not amusing, to be sure.

Ford Lee was a precise man. Even though the hole needing to be fixed was small, as was the sign, he took a great deal of time figuring out just how he was going to place it—at what angle, whether straight, slanted to the left, or to the right. He sent Buddy and Joe and me to see if we could see it from the gate while he sent the younger children, Merri, Sherri, and Terry, to tell if it could be seen from the street. Once they all determined it could indeed be read from the street—if at just a slight right slant—up it went, nailed into place for all the world to see. Now, I understood what Mama Lee meant by saying her husband was a joker.

By the time the roof was repaired, Rosie's spaghetti was heated and on the table. I showed the boys Pete's watch and told them about the inscription and all, and about Pete and how he had been a 'swell', but was still a right good fella. By his watch, it was going on seven o'clock.

Mr. Lee said grace and we all ate up, though I was still a might filled from our earlier feeding. After supper, with it still being daylight, the kids from the shantytown met out in the street for a game of stickball. There was plenty of kids to fill the bases and enough left to switch off players. Then we had us a game of hide-n-seek in the twilight. With everything I had seen in these past few weeks, it sure was good to feel like a kid again.

When Mama Lee called her children in for the night, they come a-running. Because the mud was still sticky from the morning rains, we hunkered down inside for the evening. Otherwise, on a dry warm night, the family woulda sat outside 'round a fire.

The girls brung out some yarn and tried to teach us boys how to play cat's cradle, but we was all thumbs. The littlest, Terry, was just about two-years-old and hardly able to walk without his sisters' hands. He sat on the floor and we rolled a ball back and forth, and played peek-a-boo, like I seen some of the ladies do with their babies in church when they started to fussin'.

Mr. Lee was surely a remarkable man—funny and smart. He showed us a few tricks like making a church with people inside out of our hands, and made an old frog, too. Then he told us some jokes like "Knock knock."

I was supposed to say, "Who's there?"

He says, "Red."

I says, "Red who."

And then, Mr. Lee,"Read any good books lately?"

Mr. Lee said it was a play on words. I liked it.

I told some stories about my travels—Pete, the Willises, and about Rudy being a Jew and how folks treated him badly. I left out a lot of my own story, especially about being an Angelina and thinkin' to rob the bank. I know it's all part of who I am now, but they didn't need to know it. I wasn't forgettin'. And then, Mr. Lee brung out a harmonica. Joe brung out a cigar box guitar, and Buddy showed me how he could put some paper on his comb and make it play. We clapped and sung songs until the girls and Terry fell asleep. I admit I was feeling a might tuckered too, so I asked to be excused so I could go outside and find a place to sleep before I just dropped over.

"I'll hear of no such thing, Blue," said Mama Lee. "Terry can sleep with the girls tonight and you can bunk down with Joe and Buddy."

I tried to protest, knowing how cramped for space they was, but she insisted, and so did Mr. Lee and the boys.

"Besides, Blue," said Joe, "you're leaving tomorrow for D.C., and . . . "

"And," Buddy piped in, "who knows if we'll see you again."I put my arms around their shoulders and pulled them in until our heads was all three touching.

"Sure you will," I said. "Someday."

"And don't you go sneaking off during the night or in the morning before you say goodbye," said Mama Lee, as she kissed us all goodnight. She kissed the babies, too, then joined her husband who had already gone back outside.

I heard it—their low whispers, sweet and lovely, just outside the door—as I drifted off. And I heard one last thing before sleep took me, the low WHOOO of a distant train calling.

July 8, 1937

170 Miles to go

I think I slept better than I had in all the time I'd been gone from home, not that the bed was so comfortable. The mat serving as a mattress was worn and we slept head to foot. Buddy kept sticking his foot in my face and Joe's elbow was as sharp as a knife, but the comfort come from being safe and with people I knew I could trust.

Breakfast was leftover Italian bread toasted over the wood-burning stove then spread with last autumn's canned apple butter, and washed down with strong coffee. The Lees couldn't afford sugar to cut it and really I hadn't had no sugar in so long it didn't matter. Black coffee was better than no coffee. I knowed they usually made it with used grounds but today they made it strong for me. Besides, coffee among friends is the best. Everyone in the shack was up to see me on my way.

The morning dawned sunny and warm and threatened to be a very hot July day. Mr. Lee and me carried the table and chairs into the "yard" with the mud having dried more and we ate with the birds singing in the trees across the street. If you looked east where the land slanted you could see the Delaware's blue waters glistening in the sunshine. The shantytown—I decided to call Leeville—bustled with activity as the neighbors begun their daily routines.

It turned out, some of the men did have jobs. They just didn't pay well enough to live elsewhere. Those fortunate few just tried to save up what they earned for their "someday" and used most of their pay to buy food.

Mr. Lee and the boys had a small scrap business and I reckon it made sense. He sure seemed to know where to find the good stuff, but mostly they traded what they found. There wasn't much cash-pay exchanging hands.

Joe said some of those folks was less than respectable– gambling, shoplifting, robbing. But most was kind and good. It was a small sampling of the larger city—the larger world.

"Well Blue," said Mr. Lee as he licked the remaining apple butter off his lip and drained his coffee. "It's going to be a fine day for you to travel so we better get you down to the yard. Your train comes at around 10am."

He turned to his wife. Em, you got the boy's bindle ready?"

Mrs. Lee appeared in the doorway with a small canvas flour-sack.

"Sure do, Ford. Now, Blue, this will help along the way. I wish it was more," she said. "There's a jar of canned vegetables, and you're lucky we got fresh radishes right bout now. Also," she glanced at Buddy and Joe, "well, the boys got something a little special from Giuseppe's for you, but they want it to be a surprise."

I looked at them and they was both blushing again.

"Thank you, Mama Lee. Uh, thanks fellas."

"It ain't much," said Joe.

"Tis so," argued Buddy. With a smile as big as a half-moon, he added, "You'll like it, Blue."

"Well, let's get this show on the road, fellas. Em, you and the youngins comin'?"

Mrs. Lee looked around.

"You know, we might as well. It's a nice day for a short walk. And maybe we can stop in and see Rosie on the way back. Sure."

She gathered up Merri, Sherri, and picked up Terry, then the whole family walked me to Greenwich Yard.

"We can't really go past this fence," said Mr. Lee when we come to the hole in the fence where me and the boys had popped out the day before. "Not really safe nor legal."

He looked at his wife.

"Oh go on, Ford. I'll wait here with the babies. You and the boys take this young man to his train."

Mr. Lee, Joe, Buddy, and me, ducked through the fence hole and up through between some warehouses. We wove our way along the brick walls of several buildings, under a water tower, crossed some tracks, and circled past two or three railcars. Once we made sure nobody would spot us, Mr. Lee pointed out the Washington train.

"Take that one there, Blue. It'll go all the way to Potomac Freight Yard in D.C."

I had to ask, "How'd you know which one, Mr. Lee?"

"I talk to a lot of people who ride the rails. I listen to conversations at Giuseppe's. And I got a friend on the inside." He winked.

"I sure do appreciate all you did for me, Mr. Lee. You and your wife. I reckon I plum forgot to say goodbye."

"'Round here Blue, we don't say goodbye. We just say, til next we meet."

I only nodded and shook their hands. When I did, Buddy passed me some matches.

"You might need those Blue. In case you need to build a fire."

He smiled and I was compelled to mess up his hair.

"Thanks, Pal."

"Well, we'll leave you here," said Mr. Lee. "They probably won't check the cars here in the middle of the yard. We don't get many bulls here anyway. Pick a car and get yourself set. The train'll be leavin' in a few."

I struggled not to say goodbye and not to feel sad. I was getting mighty tired of saying so long to people I liked. I just held my hand up in a wave and they waved back as they crossed over the tracks to where Mama Lee was waiting. Her and the youngins waved too.

"Til we meet again Blue! Remember!" Mr. Lee called.

I turned my back to look for a boxcar to ride and when I looked back again, the family was gone.

***

Many of the loaded cars was locked up tight, but I finally managed to find an open one and hopped in without much trouble.

I was the only rider in my car, and from what I could tell the only rider on the train that morning. I reckoned we'd pick up a few along the way. I kept myself well out of sight until the train left the yard, then I was able to peer out at some of the city along the waterfront. It was mostly industrial.

Since my car was double-doored, I was able to see some of the passing neighborhoods on the other side. Again, it was not the heart of the city, which was north of the yards. These neighborhoods also belonged to the companies along the tracks.

The industry here was not bustling. Even much of the freight yard was closed down with an open factory, warehouse, or several more boarded up buildings now and again. But the naval yards along the river, they was something else. I didn't know it at the time but the U.S.S. Cassin was born there in the naval yard and launched just the year before, along with the U.S.S. Philadelphia. Most of the thriving industry was for the naval yard. Of course, the train didn't enter in but I seen track that could be shifted to carry boxcars and gondolas filled with materials for the ships. I even seen some ships at the dock and big tall cranes for working on them. It was an amazing sight. Why that naval yard was around since the founding of the country! I made a note in my head to return there someday—who knows, maybe as a sailor on one of them ships.

Just beyond that point was a river branch feeding into the Delaware. The train slowed to cross a bridge. It was a dizzying ride, with the train rolling over the tracks, and me looking down into the water below. I decided I better have a sit-down and make myself comfortable at least until we reached the other side. The crossing didn't take so long, but right then I was feeling a little unsteady.

Mr. Lee said I'd have to ride the train all day, probably until dark before we rolled into Potomac Yard. The train had to stop every few hours to water or let another train pass going the other way. When it did, I had to hop off as it slowed and then back on when it begun to move again. Each time we stopped, a few more fellas would jump onboard. Sometimes I was able to just stay on the train, but before too long my car was getting a might crowded. Made one wonder if it was the only car available. I mean, really, with a whole darned train why did it seem everybody decided to use mine? Then again, it weren't so bad. If not for the other tramps to talk to, it woulda been a might boring ride—river, countryside, small town and more river, and more countryside. I was beginning to understand how the thrill of the journey was not what was outside the car. It was what was inside. It was the people you met along the way.

Most of the day was spent listening to these two old men who said they'd been riding the rails since they was kids and they had been all over the country—California, Texas, Arkansas, and Florida. They said they shared a boxcar with a gator in Florida! Shoot. That would be somethin'!

The other men and boys, myself included, just listened like we was sitting on our pappies' knees. Then one brought out his 'monica, and the other fella took a ukulele out of his back-sack.

They commenced to playing and we sang. Later we played some cards. I learned how to play poker, but we played for peanuts not cash money.

"And there is this big fella name of Paul Bunyan with his pal, a Blue Ox name of Babe."

One of the man just started in to telling a tale.

"No, I swear," he said, with a twinkle in his eye, "it's true. He was as tall as a tree and four times as wide. He wasn't carried by one stork when he was born, no sir, it took five!"

The fella with the uke interrupted. "No, no, no man." He was very animated and spoke with a strange accent. "You talkin' 'bout Saginaw Joe. He come down from way up Canada."

We was all laughing listening to the two of them bantering and telling tales, trying to outdo the other. I asked where they was from and what language the ukulele man was speaking, as every now and then when he got a might flustered, he commenced to speaking really fast in a language we couldn't understand. It made us laugh, all the more.

"Oh," he said. "I beg your pardon. I'm . . ." Again, he made a wide gesture placing his hand on his chest as he introduced himself, almost like he forgot he was now speaking English. "I am Michael and I am from Maine. I have French Canadian ancestry, you know Parlez vous Francais? And this . . ." He pointed at the other fella who chimed in, "My name is Ed."

Ed was from right there in Philadelphia as it turned out. He was a man of adventure—they both was. They said they just traveled around hearing tales and telling them every chance they could.

They was so expressive and so funny you couldn't help but feel good and the day passed by quicker than I knew. We all put out what food we had to share but I must confess, the little special something the boys put up for me, I kept it to myself. I ate it when nobody was looking. I didn't right know what it is called but it sure enough was the sweetest pastry I ever ate—a crispy flaky rolled up piece of dough with soft sweet creamy filling. I later found out it was called a cannoli and I never could pass them by afterward, if I had enough money.

As I ate my confection I glanced at Pete's watch. It was coming on nine o'clock and according to Mr. Lee's directions, we would be coming on to Washington. I felt my stomach jump as the train begun to slow and we seen Potomac Yard come into view.

July 9, 1937
The Capitol

"It's Pot Yard, fellas!" shouted one of men, who until then, had been fairly silent, even when he won most of the peanuts at cards. "Time to hop off!"

One thing I have found is no matter where I go, seems somebody in my company has been there before.

Tramps leapt from the train like fleas escaping from a swimming dog. The fellas scurried off for cover but the ones in my car stuck together until we found a ditch, then everybody went their own way. I tried desperately to keep up with the quiet fella, as I thought he might be able to tell me which way to get to the White House, but I lost him in the darkness. He was gone before I could blink.

I was entirely alone and it sank in like the weight on my fishing pole. I was being pulled down. I mean, there I was, standing just ten feet from some tracks, watching the train vanish into the dark. Other than that and a few other trains sitting idle in the yard, I was alone—dust on my shoes and overall legs, sweat pouring down my face and neck, squinting to see. I was not quite sure of myself, and my destination was staring me blank in the face. This was Washington D.C. but it may as well have been a dark forest full of fearsome critters, because I felt tinier than tiny, and completely lost. Thirty or so separate sets of tracks faded into shadow. That was all I could see nearby. In the distance was the lights of an enormous city—so many lights, the sky was on fire.

I stood there for a very long time when it dawned on me—not only did I not know where to begin walking, but it was nighttime in a strange place. I decided it might be best to stay put for the night, but needed someplace where I wouldn't be seen and maybe I could get some sleep.

I followed the tracks toward the city lights, which actually took me back in the direction we had come. I seen where the tracks suddenly veered off and realized those was the tracks on which boxcars was pushed around by small engines to the various buildings lining the yard. It didn't take too long to find some unhitched cars, and several more, looking like they'd seen their better days. I managed to pry open the door on one, just wide enough to crawl inside. It was empty except for a pile of old rags in one corner—a bed some hobo had left behind. I remembered my first day on the rail, when Pete and I had to run for the train and leave his hot frying pan behind. Like I said, folks leave things.

I was already dirty, head to toe, and mighty ready to drop. I crawled on top of them rags, with whatever vermin there was, and slept fairly well, exceptin' for the heat. July was wearing on and heating up fierce.

It seemed like a month had gone by since I left Selinsgrove but I knew it had only been a week or so. It didn't right matter because morning come and I was in D.C. That's all I cared about—that, and finding the White House.

***

I heard some noises out in the yard and peered through the door before leaving. There was some freight yard workers a short ways off, and so as not to be spotted, I crawled under the car to the other side. Now, by the light of day, I knew I chose the right place to spend the night. I was at the edge of the yard nearer the buildings and cover. I wove my way along a footpath in the tall grass worn by other hobos and anyone else taking a shortcut through the yard, when I come into a field overlooking the backs of several small factories and warehouses.

Poles in the field carried electrical wires and telephone lines, and I followed them in the direction of the factories. They brung me out onto a narrow street between the buildings. The street led north and was crisscrossed by other narrow streets. It was like a whole city ofindustrial buildings, and while there was workers milling about on their way to work or leaving their late shifts for home, nobody really paid me no mind. I was just a ragged boy carrying an empty flour sack tucked in his downturned overall bib. The fellas I seen was dragging their feet, and most likely thought me to be one of them.

The streets around the factories was parked with theoccasional automobile—most likely belongin' to the boss men. The average man walked or took a bus. All I knew was I needed to find my way out of this maze.

"'Scuse me, sir," I said, getting the attention of one of the men leaving a building. "Can you tell me how to find the White House?"

It was like I asked him to give me a million dollars. He give me such a look.

"Well, son," he chuckled, placing his cap on his head. "You're a might far from the White House. It's almost six miles that way." He pointed northwest. "Across the river."

I felt my heart sink. It was a two-hour walk if I knew the way, and without any buildings in my path. Like they say, as the crow flies. But that weren't the case, and I weren't no crow.

I thanked the man, then added, "Is there a diner nearby?"

"Up three blocks," he said with a nod.

I was grateful it was the same direction I was heading, as I was feeling hungry. I didn't want my time with the First Lady to be filled with my stomach growling. Besides, I still had three dollars from Mr. Willis.

Most of the way to the diner was one small factory after another—some in use, others empty. Once I got within one block of the diner, I begun to see houses lining the street. They was all the same—two story with upper and lower flats. Each had a small balcony for the upper, or else, the residences was side by side with three steps going up to each door. I knew this was company-owned from some of the conversation with Mr. Lee about the housing situation in the cities. He said folks was lucky if they lived where their employer was landlord these days. It cost too much to own it yerself. The downside, though, was if folks lost their work, they was out on the street. It weren't Mr. Lee's case but he knew a few folks who had it happen to them.

Near the end of the next block, just across the street, was Walter's grocery. It was still closed but I figured on stopping in after I had a warm breakfast. At the corner, I started seeing a mix of what looked like single-family homes and small businesses flanking the street. Then, I seen Mom's Diner. The name was sweet, but by the looks of it, the diner was a bona fide "greasy spoon." The entrance was at street level. Two dirty windows sat to either side of the door, with soiled café curtains hanging askew. In fact, most of the last three blocks had blackened windows—I reckon from the factory smoke. When I opened the door, a little bell on a spring rang and the factory workers having breakfast turned to look. When they realized I wasn't somebody they knew, they resumed their talking and eating.

It was a small place with booths up one wall and a counter with stools on the other side, beyond which was the grill and kitchen. I took an empty stool at the counter. It squeaked as I sat. The last fella's empty dish and dirty cup was still sitting there with a dime he left the waitress for tip. When I took my seat she seemed to appear out of no place, swooping in like a hawk, scooping up the dirty dishes and dime in one move. She looked me over.

The waitress had teased up hair, about as blond as I ever seen. I figured it weren't her real color, but who am I to judge? The fellas woulda called her a "bale of straw." She wore a tight blue and white checkered uniform with a little frilled apron, fairly soiled. The hem just barely made it to her knees. Her nametag said her name was Lucille.

Lucille wore a lot more makeup than I ever seen on one woman, and reddish lipstick. She looked pretty old, at least thirty, but it mighta been the get-up made her look older. She had "beanery queen" written all over her, from what I heard other 'bos say about the waitresses in these railroad eateries.

Lord knows I tried to adopt the hobo-lingo but it just didn't spill off my tongue. If it had, I woulda asked the factory worker for a beanery and not a diner. I don't know if it's a good thing or not, really. I guess I liked the way it sounded though. Then, it dawned on me—I could order in hobo-speak! It was a whole other language, a lot like the "inscription" on Pete's watch, I suppose.

"Whatcha havin', sweetie?" She snapped the gum she was chewing.

I didn't have time to look over the menu but I mostly knew what I wanted.

"Adam and Eve on a raft, and a pile-driver, please." I blushed when the words come out.

"Why, ain't you about the cutest thang?" she said. "But you better show me the do-re-mi."

She waited, tapping her foot and rolling her eyes, and kind of doing this little dancing wiggle like she was hearing music in her head.

I took out my coin and showed I was good for it—all 35 cents! Then she smiled, and shouted over to the cook, "Two eggs on toast!" To me she said, "And one strong coffee, black, comin' up, Blue Eyes."

Lucille wiggled off to fetch my coffee, and I reached over for a newspaper sitting on the counter. Right there, in big bold letters over a photograph of a woman in a flying get-up, was the headline:

Renowned Flyer Amelia Earhart Remains Missing

I recalled Pa talking about a big ole gas-filled flying machine crashing in May, and we talked about it in school, too. I think it was called The Hindenburg, and it was a dirigible full of hydrogen. Yes, that was it.

Now this woman went missing? I was just eight-years-old when she become the first woman to fly a plane across the ocean. I remember Mama saying how she wished she had a daughter who might do something like that, and Pa chimed in, "*Well, Missus, maybe our Billy will be the flyer in the family. You never can tell.*"

Wonder if Mama heard about this aeroplane going down? The paper said Earhart was flying over the Pacific this time.

"Hey, Lucille . . ."

"I'm bringing your java now," she said.She set the mug down and pushed a spoon at me rather brusquely.

"No disrespect, Miss. I was just wondering if you knew the name of the other ocean."

"What you talking about?"

"Well, this paper says Amelia Earhart is missing over the Pacific." I had to sound the words out carefully, as my reading still wasn't too good, but I could tell a bit from the picture. "I was wondering what the other ocean is called. I can't remember."

Almost at the same time, all the other fellas in the place shouted, "ATLANTIC!"

I felt a bit foolish so I covered by making Lucille a compliment. "I bet you could fly a plane if you wanted."

It mighta been more foolish than not knowing the name of the Atlantic—which, by the way, I never forgot again—but it made Lucille smile.

"Thanks, kid."

She turned as the cook called, "Adam and Eve!"

Bringing me my eggs, she touched the top of my hand as she set down the plate.

"You're all right, Blue Eyes. What you doing here in Washington? You ain't been in here before. You a tramp?"

By then, I was already shoveling food in my mouth, drunk a slug of coffee, and took another bite to boot. My mouth was full, as I replied, "Going to see the First Lady."

Well now I done it. I brung the house down with laughter. I just hung my head in shame and kept on eating. Though I didn't have the same appetite I had coming in, there was no telling when I'd stop at another diner, so I ate up.

Once the laughter subsided, Lucille come a little closer and said, "Sugar, you know how to find the White House?"

"Nope."

"Well, you're gonna have to walk awhile, but just keep heading with the Potomac on your right." She motioned north. "You gotta cross some bridges, but you'll come to the city. Then you'll have to ask somebody else, but you'll find it. Do me a favor, will ya? Tell the First Lady for me, I think she's doing a fine job."

I smiled at her. "I will. Thanks for not laughing."

"Blue Eyes, I had a dream once, too. You do it for me."

I finished eating, and when Lucille weren't looking, I slipped a dime under my plate. I couldn't afford the tip, Lord knows, but I had a feeling she needed it. Mama woulda said it was the right thing to do.

I walked back to Walter's and bought some apples from the bins in front of the grocery, and a can of pork and beans. It cost me another dime, but I was used to stretching a meal. I reckoned it would get me through a couple days at least, especially if I could find a breadline. There had to be one someplace in the Capitol.

I did as Lucille suggested and kept on walking north. It couldn'ta been more than a mile, maybe less, when I come to a water outlet into the Potomac. Two or three miles more, and I come to another. I didn't know what it was but I knew I had to cross it. I checked now and then with folks I seen and they just kept pointing me northward, so I knowed I was in the right place. Fact is, this was the very same railroad bridge I just crossed the night before, only I didn't know we had crossed water in the dark. It brung me out on a strip of land surrounded by water.

On the island, there was a stretch of promenade. Leastwise, Mama used to call long walkways 'promenades.' There was trees and flowers planted all along the way. I seen folks strolling, and I reckon they was folks who didn't have to work and didn't need to worry about it.

As I was walking along, a stick landed at my feet. It kind of flew out of no place. I looked to see if it dropped from a tree, then picked it up. When I did, there was a sweet little dog at my feet, staring at the stick and panting furiously.

"Sorry, Mister," said a small boy. "I didn't mean to hit ya. I'm a bad shot. I meant that for Mr. Blinky."

"Mr. Blinky?" I asked, laughing. "That your dog? Why do you call him Blinky? Looks more like a Shaggy to me."

"Cuz his hair gets in his eyes and he blinks."

"Okay, kid," I said, holding up the stick. "Here you go, Mr. Blinky. Fetch!"

I threw the stick a distance off, but not too far so the little boy could keep up with his dog, and off they went.

I seen some folks with picnic baskets at the water's edge, and I seen a lady strolling her baby. Now she walked right by me, and I reckon I couldn't help but look inside. I do believe it was the ugliest kid I ever seen, but of course, I didn't tell her. All I said was

"Fine day," and kept a-goin'. Mama always said, we was all God's creatures, and we all looked beautiful to Him and to our mammas. I had to chuckle right then, until I felt Mama tug on my ear. She had a way of reminding me, even when she weren't there.

The sound of laughing children knocked me out of another one of my daydreams. Several children, all under the eagle-eyes of three women dressed in plain clothes, stood out in a shallow span of water, splashing around and having a fine old time. I really wanted to join them but I didn't see no other growed people out there in the water. It sure looked mighty tempting on such a hot day, only I didn't want no trouble with the law. I was thinking I was too close to my destination to be stopped. That's when I seen it. Right there across the water, standing straight and tall like a beacon, was a white tower.

"Ma'am?" I absentmindedly reached out and tugged the sleeve of one the ladies watching the children. She give me a glare.

"I mean, excuse me. What is that white tower over there."

Her eyes followed my finger.

"Boy, that's the Washington Monument."

"And how far am I from the White House?"

"Oh, I think you are about two miles."

She musta thought I gone loco. I throwed my cap in the air and jumped off the ground. "HEEEE OWWWW!!! I'm almost there!"

I seen the ladies jump with a start and the kids' splashing stopped. Everybody in hearing distance turned to see this crazy boy dancing around in a circle.

"I'm almost there, Mama!"

Then I seen an officer in uniform swinging his stick, talking to somebody across the green. He blowed a whistle and begun to stride toward me at a fast pace. I picked my cap up right quick, thanked the ladies, and run off. Over my shoulder, I seen the officer go back to his chat.

The White House

Crossing the bridges from Potomac Yard to D.C. seemed to take forever when actually, it took about thirty minutes.

The white tower—the Washington Monument—was my lighthouse showing me the way. I walked toward it, and as long as it was there in front of me, I knew I was traveling in the right direction.

I glanced at Pete's watch. It was going on noon. Musta been why I seen so many men and women leaving buildings. They was probably going for their lunch. I figured it wouldn't be bad for me to sit a spell and have a bite, but I was too excited, and frankly, I still couldn't see the White House. I wanted to see it more than anything.

I walked just a few long city blocks past several of the biggest buildings I ever seen. They weren't so tall, but I swear, they was as large as our whole town! Then I come to a wide avenue and almost got run over by the automobiles. I never seen so many in one place, and so many people! Looking up the avenue to the east, I seen a long expanse of trees and more of them large buildings. That must be how the city of Rome looked all them years ago. The trees, the people—everything looked like ants next to them big buildings. And there in the distance, with its white dome gleaming in the noon sun, was the Capitol building. I seen pictures of it, but I never imagined the immense power it would have over me, seeing it right now for real. I mighta been dreaming.

There was all these museums, too. I surely wished I coulda took a look-see. And a big ole castle! Whoever expected to see a castle in the middle of Washington? My teacher never said there was castles here. She only said kings and queens used to live in castles. I knew we didn't have no royal-folk in our country. I was perplexed. I took off my cap, scratched my head, and give a low whistle.

"Are you lost, son?"

The sudden sound of a voice startled me and I reckon I jumped. Turning around, I seen a fine lady carrying shopping bags. Wisps of white hair just showed from under a straw cloche, and she wore a light blue and white flowered frock with a string of pearls round her neck. She looked about my mama's age.

"Well now, Ma'am," I replied, "I think I know where I am, but maybe you can tell me what that there castle is doing in the middle of the city? Is it part of some show?"

She smiled. "The Castle, as we call it, is the main building for the Smithsonian Institution."

"Smithso . . . so . . . "

"Smithsonian. All these buildings here are part of the museum complex." She made a short sweeping gesture with her hand.

"You mean to tell me these buildings are full of pictures and old stuff from when my granddaddy was alive?"

"Something like that," she replied. "This is our country, right here, in these buildings. If you want to know anything about who we are, where we came from, and what we've done, it's here on display."

I let out a whistle again. "I never."

"It's an amazing place. Are you going in?"

I shook my head. "No, I . . . I can't right now. I'm going to the White House. Can you tell me where to find it?"

Again, she smiled—this time with a wider grin.

"Can I tell you where to find it?" She took my arm. "Come with me."

We turned around and paced west down the avenue, and there was the Washington Monument. If it looked mighty before, it looked mightier right there in the center of a circular green. It pointed straight up to heaven, like it was poking God and saying, *"Look down here God, see what we did."* I almost swallowed my heart when I seen it up close. We walked down the street and crossed over when traffic was clear.

The avenue was a pretty street with all them trees and plenty of flowers. The circular green was right pretty, too. It was crowded with people who come just to see the city and its sights. I reckoned some was working close by and now was having their lunches. Others sat outdoors reading the newspaper or a book.

Once we got out onto the green patch, the woman told me to look northward. I believe I did swallow my heart that time, as way up north of the green—shining like a palace fit for royalty—was the White House. My heart commenced to leaping out of my throat.

"Lady, I come a long way to see that building. You can't imagine what I went through to get here. And I thank you kindly for showing me the way. Now, I gotta leave you because I need to go see Mrs. Roosevelt."

"Whoa, there, son." She placed a hand on my arm, not rough but kindly. "You say you're going to see the First Lady?"

"Yes, Ma'am, I am."

"You can't just go barging into the White House to meet her. You need an appointment. Besides, Mrs. Roosevelt isn't there right now."

"Well, I can wait to see her. They must have a place for folks to wait."

"Why, yes, they do. But right now, Mrs. Roosevelt is away in New York."

Now, I was stunned. It felt like somebody punched me in the stomach, and I kind of lost my balance—felt a little dizzy.

"I think you better sit down, dear," she said.

I let myself drop onto a bench and she sat next to me.

"When was the last time you had something to eat?"

I didn't hear her, with the blood pounding in my ears.

"Son," she placed her hand on my arm again.

"Yes, Ma'am. I mean, no, Ma'am. What did you ask?"

"When did you last eat?"

"Oh, I ate this morning."

"Well, from the looks of you, you better have some lunch. Do you have something to eat in your sack?"

She reached over and opened the flour sack I had let fall to the ground.

"Is this all you have? Two apples and a can of beans?"

"I reckon it should do," I replied.

"Nonsense. Where are you from? Are you here alone? With a school group? Family?"

There was more questions than I could answer, so all I said was, "Alone, I reckon."

"You better sit here a spell, until you get your legs again. What is your name?"

I told her my proper name was William Saxton, "But most folks call me Blue."

"Blue, it is then, and I see why."

She held out a soft hand to shake and I tried not to squeeze it too hard.

"Marguerite LeHand. Now, why don't you tell me why you are so eager to meet Mrs. Roosevelt."

"Well, Ma'am, see, I wrote a letter to Mrs. Roosevelt. My folks are mighty poor and my pa is . . . was mighty sick. Truth is, I don't even know if he is still alive." Miss Lehand's eyes widened, then her brows knit. "I asked Mrs. Roosevelt for some chicken soup and one of her castoff dresses for my mama. She sure could use one. Leastwise, that was why I wrote. When she didn't write back, I decided to come tell her in person, only, Ma'am, I've seen so much on my way here. I reckon I got another reason to see her now. Now, I want her to know about the folks I met and the things I seen. I got messages for her and the president from lots of folks."

"My goodness, Blue, you carry a heavy load for such a young man. Why, right now, the president is lunching with the Ambassador of China, and I expect he hasn't got as much to say as you have. You're quite an ambassador, yourself. It's commendable." She bit her lip. "I'm truly sorry you didn't receive a reply from Mrs. Roosevelt, but I have to tell you, the Roosevelts get hundreds of letters, like yours, every week. Unemployment dropped, but is on the rise again. There are so many still out of work. And, do you know," she began, as she shooed away some pigeon's looking for a hand-out, "when the president took office, almost one quarter of the country's population was unemployed? And we estimate, over the past seven years, almost one hundred fifty thousand young people like you have been on the road. It's a staggering number. President and Mrs. Roosevelt barely have time to catch their breaths, but they try to answer all those letters, Blue. I know they do."

I was stunned. I knew there was lots of folks hurting. I met plenty of 'em, but I never imagined so many.

"So that's why she didn't write. But it don't matter no more 'cause . . . " I put my hand over a spot of Shorty's blood on my overalls. "I know now it was wrong to ask her for help. We need to do for ourselves the best we can. See, I met a lot of folks on my journey and I want to tell Mrs. Roosevelt about them, so really, I just gotta see her for a little while."

"Are you feeling a bit better now? Can you take a walk with me?" Miss LeHand asked.

"Well, yes, Ma'am, I do feel better. I still think I should go to the White House and see for myself."

"If you can walk, Blue, I'll take you there."

She give me her arm to steady me and we walked up toward the White House. "And here," she said, pulling one of the apples from my sack, "you better eat this while we walk."

"Thank you, Ma'am." I hesitated but I had to ask, "I wonder, Ma'am, how is it you know so much about what is going on in the White House? Do they put all that in the newspaper?"

"Yes, they do print much of it, Blue. The American people have a right to know what their leaders are doing. But . . . well, I know because I work in the White House."

I stopped D-E-A-D in my tracks and turned to face her.

"You work in the White House? Ma'am, you wouldn't be funning me, would you?"

"No, Blue, I'm not funning you. I am Mr. Roosevelt's social secretary."

And it weren't like she was bragging, neither. She didn't miss a step and I had to catch up with her.

"So, where are we going, Ma'am?"

"I'm taking you to my office, but first we will stop at the kitchen to get you something proper to eat. And afterward, you are going to write another letter to Mrs. Roosevelt." And now, she stopped walking to look at me, then added, "And I promise she will read it, Blue, and reply. I'll hand it to her personally."

I went all speechless because right about then, I looked up and seen we was standing at the White House gate. The apple core fell from my hand and rolled under a bush. I ain't never seen such a grand entrance and such a large lawn. Reckon my jaw dropped.

The Fast "Train" Home

I listened to too many tales down at the barbershop. Somehow, in my imagination, I thought everybody who wanted to get into the White House—who wasn't part of the family or in office—might have to be blindfolded so as not to know how they got inside or where they was going. But no. Miss LeHand and me walked right around to the staff gate, which weren't the same one the dignified folk used—though I thought Miss LeHand was mighty dignified—and we went right to the kitchen. 'Course, she had to be recognized by a guard at the gate, and explain who I was.

I don't expect I ever have, or ever will be in, such a grand kitchen again. Why, they had cooks and servants wearing white coats and caps and all busy, with one thing or another, but it seemed nobody had to do it all. I wondered what mama woulda said! I seen Mama, when we used to have money for bigger meals, scurrying from the stove to the icebox to the table. But here in the White House kitchen, they had stainless steel countertops and tables, and lots of people to do the work. In fact, Miss LeHand said it was a brand new kitchen—only a couple years old. She said Mrs. Roosevelt's housekeeper couldn't stand how dirty the old one was, so they just built it new. Imagine. Why, I counted no less than six ovens, a huge stove bigger than my bedroom was long, eight refrigerators, and five dishwashers—not the human kind but the machine kind. There was all these grinders for meat, irons for making waffles, more than one mixer, and an enormous freezer.

Why, I seen a fella walk into the freezer. He said it was for keeping the ice cream! But best of all, there was all these elevators for taking food to different floors. Mrs. LeHand called them 'dumbwaiters.'

"Mrs. Nesbitt–that's the housekeeper's name–is at Hyde Park with Mrs. Roosevelt. But, I'm certain we can still get you something to eat. Isn't that right, Ingrid?" she said turning to one of the servants busily laying out pastries on a baking sheet.

"Yes, Ma'am," the servant replied, and she almost disappeared in the mess of refrigerators. But, when she returned she brought a tray with a bowl of cold soup–since it was summer, and a side of green beans, and a glass of milk.

"Now, you sit right here, Blue," said Miss Lehand. "I think this will be more comfortable for you than my office. I won't be long, but take your time."

She pulled out a chair and I sat at the table. The servant placed the tray in front of me. I thanked Ingrid, and Miss LeHand who left me in the care of the kitchen staff.

I could feel their eyes burning holes in the back of my head, and while I could hear them whispering, I couldn't make out what they was saying. Then I heard a man clear his throat and the chattering stopped. It was replaced by the sound of pans and plates as staff moved about in their routines.

While I never had thought soup should be cold, it sure tasted mighty good. By the time Miss LeHand returned, I was finished and actually starting to get fidgety.

"I hope I didn't keep you waiting too long, Blue. Here."

She set some writing paper on the table along with a fountain pen and an envelope. They was sure finer than anything we used in school. I felt like a real swell.

"I want you to write whatever you wish to say to Mrs. Roosevelt and seal it in the envelope. I won't even read it, but I will make sure she gets it as soon as she returns."

After a bit, I commenced to writing.

Dear Mrs. Roosevelt:

My name is William Saxton, but most folks call me Blue. I left home many days ago to come and see you about the letter I sent before. In it, I asked for chicken soup because we don't have much food, and my pa has been mighty sick. And I asked for any old clothes you might have for my mama. But, Ma'am, that's not why I am writin' now.

When I left home, I was sixteen-years-old and I am still sixteen but I will be seventeen soon. I know they take boys for the Civilian Conservation Corp at seventeen and I mean to join up as soon as I get home. That way, I can help my family the way it oughta be done. You and Mr. Roosevelt begun the CCC for just such a reason and I want to thank you.

I am also writin' because I got things to tell you about what I seen and messages from some of the folks I met.

I don't know if you fine folks know the kind of people who live in this here beautiful country. I kinda reckon you do. But there's also a lot of bad people, Mrs. Roosevelt. I met fellas who would sooner skin ya alive than look at ya sidewise. I met fellas who take advantage of those who are weak, or hate others simply because they are different. But the good news is, there are far more kind folk.

I went on to tell Mrs. Roosevelt about Pete, and how his business failed but he had a courage deep inside and wouldn't give up. How he was trying to make things work with his old business partner. I told her about the young people I met, Fred and Penny, and how their folks abused them and they had to take care of themselves. And, about Shorty and other kids getting killed riding the rails. And, about the Willises who was happy to give a poor stranger a leg up, and how the Lees had nothing, but had everything all at the same time.

And Ma'am, I have a message from a waitress over at Mom's Diner. She says you are doing a fine job and that is helping her to find her dreams again.

So, Mrs. Roosevelt, I don't need the soup no more, nor the clothes, because I'm gonna find a way to buy them on my own. And someday, I'm gonna finish school, and I think I will do something for my country.

Thanks, kindly, to you and the President.

Regards,

William Saxton

I done as Miss LeHand said, and folded the letter and sealed it up, then handed her the envelope. She placed it in her dress pocket and took out another envelope.

"Have you ever ridden a Greyhound Motor Coach, Blue?"

It took me a minute to understand what she was asking.

"No, Ma'am, I ain . . . er . . . *have* . . .not."

"Well, this is a ticket to take you home, Blue. I would have given you some cash, too, but I expect you are the kind of young man who does not accept charity unless absolutely needed. Am I right?"

"Yes, Ma'am! And I rightly don't know what to say but, I reckon I got here and would be all right getting myself home."

"I know you would, Blue, but I want you to think of your mother. How do you think she would feel if I just open the kitchen door and send you off on your way, all these miles from home in a strange city?"

I understood, as Mama would not have thought well on it. I took the ticket, gratefully.

"I thank you, Ma'am, and I want you know, when I can, I will repay your kindness."

"It isn't necessary, Blue. The President would want me to do this, too. And somehow, I think maybe you'll give back to your country someday."

"I aim to, Ma'am."

She smiled and asked Ingrid to pack some extra food in my flour sack. Then she asked the fella, who had cleared his voice earlier, to have the staff car brung ‘round. He mighta been a butler by the way he was suited up.

“This is where I leave you, Blue, in the capable hands of our driver, John. He will take you to the depot where you can catch your Greyhound. Just show your ticket when you get there and someone will help you find the correct motor coach.”

She held out her soft hand again.

“It has been a pleasure, William Saxton.”

“For me, too,” I said. And I thanked the kitchen folks, especially Ingrid. “That was some bowl-lickin’ good soup.”

Everybody laughed, as I reckon I didn’t say it the way they woulda, butno mind, I was happy to be going home.

Riding in Style

John, the White House staff driver, took me to the depot by way of what he called the "scenic drive." He pointed out some of the sights I already seen, and a few I hadn't, like the Lincoln Memorial. It was almost more than I could take in.

When we arrived at the terminal, he dropped me off at the doors and waited for me to enter the building. I reckon Miss LeHand mighta been worried I wouldn't take the motor coach and that I might even sell my ticket. Maybe there's plenty who woulda done it, but I surely appreciated her generosity and the comfort of going home in style. Only, I didn't plan to ride the Greyhound all the way.

The terminal was about as sleek as I reckon I ever seen, except for the White House kitchen. There was so much chrome and bright colors, I think a fella could go blind looking at it too long. I don't rightly know what it all reminded me of, but I was thinking of outer space, like I heard some fellas talking about. My imagination played with the thought but my sensibility said it ain't never gonna happen—spaceships and the like. No, sir, not with so many problems to solve right here. But the terminal and the bus was a sight. The long bus held a lot of people, like a train car, only, on the road. I liked the look of the big ole running dog painted the side. That's why they call it a Greyhound, I guess, after a dog that can run so fast. Mama was going to love hearing about all this, if she ever spoke to me again after what I done.

I hadn't thought on Mama too much of late. I been so glamoured by all I seen. How was I gonna find the courage to face her, and how was it gonna be if Pa had died while I was gone? I suddenly realized the great burden I had left her with when I run off.

It was already four o'clock in the afternoon when I heard my destination called over the loudspeaker. After waiting in a fairly long line of people, who was going home after seeing the Capitol, I took a window seat. I wasn't gonna miss a minute of the sights as we drove off—no, sir.

"Is this seat taken?"

A lady carrying a baby, and a suitcase—she didn't want to leave stowed beneath in the luggage locker—waited in the aisle.

"No, Ma'am," I replied.

"Would you mind?"

She actually handed her baby to me!

"Oh, Ma'am, no. I ain't never held . . . "

But it was too late. The baby was in my lap squirming and whimpering for his mama. Another fella helped her lift her case to the overhead, then she took the aisle seat next to me while reaching for the baby in one motion.

"Thank you. I'm sorry to impose but . . . "

"That's all right, Ma'am."

"You going far? We're going to Harrisburg to see my family. They haven't seen the baby yet, and he's almost a year old."

"That's nice." I smiled. "I'm going to Selinsgrove."

"That's nice," she said.

Then she turned her full attention back on her child, and I once more looked out the window. The motor coach engines revved up and we was underway. I must say, it was a comfort not to have to run alongside it to jump onboard. And I enjoyed watching the scenery instead of a clapboard boxcar wall.

***

We stopped about six o'clock so folks could use the restrooms and buy their meals at a diner. Already, we was in Pennsylvania again, having made a few stops along the way. I stretched my legs a piece, but with breakfast at Mom's and lunch at the White House, I reckon I wasn't too hungry. I did look in the flour sack to see what they put in there. There was some fresh fruit, a liverwurst sandwich, a bologna sandwich, and some fresh-baked peanut butter cookies. I ate a cookie and I knew I wasn't gonna be hungry at all until I got home. I asked the driver where we was and he said it was Lancaster.

"Do you stop in Selinsgrove?"

"Yes, son. We'll be there by tomorrow noon."

I suppose I didn't think it was gonna take another half day but there was stops to make, and he said we had to layover the night in Harrisburg, our next stop.

It was close to eight by the time we arrived in Harrisburg. As we pulled into the terminal, I seen a small army of about fifteen people standing and waving as the lady sitting next to me disembarked. Again I held her baby while she got her case. I watched through the window as she was surrounded by her family with hugs and kisses and ogles for that baby of hers. I wondered if she knew how lucky she was. I think maybe she did.

The driver said we was all getting off here until morning. Those who wanted to could go to the motel nearby and the rest could sleep in the terminal. I reckon I knew where I was sleeping. I found a bench nobody was using and spread myself out with my cap and flour sack for a pillow, but I decided against using the sack because I didn't want to crush my sandwiches. It didn't take me long to fall asleep at all. I was plum tuckered. And I dreamed for the first time in a while.

July 10-24, 1937

One More Stop

"Selinsgrove, Pennsylvania!" The sound caused me to jump. That was my stop!

The passengers in the Harrisburg depot had risen early. I ate my liverwurst sandwich and a pear, then we boarded our coach. By then, it was nearly 9:30am. I never had the need to measure time so much, but having Pete's watch and a serious desire to be underway, well, I kept a-glancing at it. Just like the driver said, after making several stops, it was coming on noon. He called out my destination again.

"Selinsgrove! Anybody for Selinsgrove?"

"Me, sir!"

A man who had boarded in Harrisburg blocked my way to the aisle, so he had to move to let me out. I felt the bus slowing, and it struck me again how nice it was not to have to leap off a movin' train. It was hard to keep my footing as I walked up the aisle, but as soon as the bus come to a complete stop, I was able to move better.

"Anybody else?" the driver called to the back. "No? All right,then. Here you go, son. Watch your step."

The driver moved the handle and the door swung open, and there I was, looking out the door at the moving picture theater. They didn't have a proper Greyhound terminal so the theater doubled as a stop, and anybody wanting to ride would be waiting there. I was the only person getting off and nobody was getting on.

I climbed down the bus steps to the sidewalk, then turned and waved as the driver closed the door and the coach drove off. I didn't even know what day it was but I knew where I wanted to go first thing—the general store.

I seen a few folks milling about on the green, enjoying the beautiful July afternoon. A couple fellas had a game of horseshoes going, so I figured it must be Saturday. I do believe one of them recognized me, because he waved. I couldn't tell who he was, but I waved back.

I paused outside the general store. The sidewalk beneath the overhang was dirty with some straw—most likely from some of the crates of goods being opened. As usual, there was a broom leaning up against the building, and instinctively, I picked it up and begun to sweep.

"Who's sweeping?" I heard Mr. Willis call, as he walked toward the door. "Mighty neighborly . . . " Mr. Willis stopped in stride. "Well, I don't believe it. Blue! is that you?"

I turned and held out my hand. "Yes, sir!"

I got an unexpected hug instead of a handshake, but it was fine with me. Mr. Willis held me off a bit to give me the once-over.

"Why, you're a sight for sore eyes, son. What are you doing back here?"

"Well, sir, I been to D.C."

"You made it? Oh, how splendid. Come in out of this sun, Blue, and tell me all about it."

We walked inside the store and I paused to take in the smell I loved so much.

"Nothin' changed, sir, 'cept maybe some of your dry goods."

"Blue, it's only been a couple weeks, but yes, I am always moving things around. You know, it helps bring different merchandise to folks' attention. Now, tell me, what happened in Washington? Did you see the First Lady? The president?"

"Well, not quite Sir. I seen the president's own secretary but not Mrs. Roosevelt. You're gonna think this is funny—I was taken aback, but now I look on it and think it was funny, too. She wasn't even in Washington. She was in New York City!"

"Well, I'll be," Mr. Willis said, wiping sweat from his forehead with an old hankie he took from his back pocket. "So, what did you do, and what brings you back here?"

"I wrote another letter and give it to Miss LeHand, the secretary, and come back here to work, sir. That is, before I go home. I gotta go home, but I want to take some cash money with me. If you'll have me."

"Mrs. Willis is going to be so pleased to see you. And Blue, of course you can work for me. I can't pay more than before, I hope you understand. Things are still somewhat difficult."

"I understand, sir, and I won't be no trouble. Speaking of trouble, sir," I said, shifting my weight and chewed my lip, uncertain if I really wanted to know the answer, but I asked, "what happened to Mack and Lou, and the bunch at the jungle?"

"No trouble, Blue. You'll come stay with us, of course. As for Mack and his gang, the sheriff picked them up for questioning, and searched the jungle, which they could do since those men was squatters on private property. They found plenty of evidence in Mack's shack. Only, they had them a good lawyer. Not a good man, but a good lawyer."

"Hanson," I said with a frown. *The no-good skunk who belonged to the KKK, He musta decided to defend them for no good reason of his own, I'm sure.*

"That's right. He took their case and managed to get an order to have the whole trial moved, on account of Selinsgrove being prejudiced toward the lot of them. He tried to have charges removed, due to there being no witnesses."

"But I give the report to the police. You was with me!"

"No matter. They couldn't bring you into court, so it's been moved. But don't you worry none. Once the sheriff arrested the gang and gathered the evidence, other boys came forward. It was just too late for a trial here in Selinsgrove. They'll get what's coming to them."

"What about Hanson?"

"Nobody has seen hide nor hair of him or his rotten kid since he took the case. He cleared out his office and house, and moved closer to the trial city. Going to try the gang in Harrisburg."

"It seems rash, moving like that."

"Well, not really, Blue. Hanson hasn't been too popular around here for some time. Then, after you left, so did his wife. Plus, somebody started sending threats and calling their house. I think he decided it was better to pick up and skedaddle. It's been a more peaceful, lovely, town since he left, too."

I was happy to hear all those bad folks was gone from Selinsgrove, but I worried they had just moved someplace else—especially the Hansons.

It sure was good to have my job back again, even if it was only going to be a couple weeks. And it was right nice of the Willises to let me stay at their place, since now, they knew me. I didn't refuse, and this time, I worked all the way through when I promised.

***

My birthday was July 13 and Mrs. Willis baked me a whole cake, with candles and everything. They sung Happy Birthday and give me a couple gifts. I did not expect that—no, sir. Mrs. Willis give me a real pair of trousers and a new white shirt, she said was for dressing up proper, and some new socks. Mr. Willis give me my very own razor, mug, and brush, as he said he believed I was sprouting some peach fuzz. I *was* seventeen now.

During those two weeks, all I could do was think about going home, but I knew I wanted to earn money first.

The highlight, though, had to be a date with my strawberry cloud, Elizabeth. I swear, she still smelled like strawberries.

We went to a motion picture show and seen this adventure film *Captains Courageous*. It was about this boy on a ship who got swept overboard and picked up by a fishing boat. His whole life changed, and I couldn't help but think about my own adventure and wonder if it would make a good movie. Elizabeth let me hold her hand during the show, and on the way home, too!

She told me she planned on going to college the following year, but she promised to write. We exchanged addresses, and I do hope she'll keep her promise. I guess I gotta say, though I blush telling it, I got my first kiss, and well, I still taste it too. I really do love strawberries.

With most of my three dollars and now another six more, it was time to say goodbye to the Willises again, and to Elizabeth, and Selinsgrove—maybe for good this time.

Mr. Willis asked how I was getting home and I said I reckoned I'd be hopping on the next freight train. When Mrs. Willis heard it, she turned pale.

"Henry Willis?"

Mrs. Willis was looking at her husband, and she had that 'look' again. You could not refuse that woman, no how.

"Yes, well,what my wife wants me to tell you, is we have arranged a special escort for you, Blue. We want to be sure you get home safely. Sheriff Smith has agreed to send a car with an officer to drive you home."

I wanted to balk. There was no way I wanted to even come near a police car or have anyone escorting me, but there was no arguing. It was what it was.

Mr. Willis phoned up the police station and they sent the car over. Mrs. Willis knew it wasn't gonna take more than a couple hours to get there by car, but she packed me a lunch, nonetheless, and something for the officer, too. She wasn't there to say goodbye, just like she wasn't there before. She suddenly found something she needed to do in town, but Mr. Willis was there, with a hug and a handshake.

"You know, Blue . . . "

"I know, sir. Thank you."

We pulled away from the store and drove 'cross town. I watched as the green with its bandstand disappeared in the distance, and I seen the tracks coming up in front of us. We slowed to make sure no trains was coming, then crossed over, and I was on my way home. The officer doing the driving was nice enough, but not big on conversation so the trip was fairly quiet.

We was many miles down the road, when I looked in the sack Mrs. Willis give me. She couldn't be there to say goodbye, but she did leave me a note.

Dearest William,

If I were to have a second son, God rest my boy's soul, I would want him to be you. Your mother must be a very fine lady to have raised such an upstanding young man.

Mr. Willis and I truly loved having you with us. Please remember us, William, as we will remember you, and I hope you will write and let us know what you are doing.

Sincerely,

Dolores

P.S. I meant to write "with love."

I folded the note and placed it carefully in my pocket, determined never to lose it. I would remember them. I would remember them all.

Home At Last

My greatest relief was when Mama took me in her arms. I felt mighty fortunate–like the lady with the baby in Harrisburg–to have someone love me so much. There was no scolding or strap, and no Pa. He was alive, but Mama said the doctor had insisted on taking him north for treatments. She said she got a letter just the other day saying he might be coming home in about a month. It was mighty expensive, and I offered to help when I found some work, but Mama said no. She had received an anonymous donation. Well, my curiosity was piqued but nobody could say who give the money. It was a complete mystery.

It took some time to get 'round to telling Mama the story about my adventures and the folks I met. I expected her to lecture me on all the things I done wrong, but instead, Mama smiled.

"I'm mighty proud of you, Billy, and your pa will be, too. Now, don't get me wrong." Her smiled vanished and was replaced by a stern look. "I do not condone your running away ever again, but everything else is all right. Except of course . . . "

All right, now it was comin' for sure. All I dreaded was wrapped in that one pause.

"Except for missing your birthday. You left here a boy and have returned a man. It's not just your age, neither. It's your way of carrying yourself. You carry yourself like a fine gentleman." Mama wiped a tear. "I really don't think any mother could be more proud than I am, and I am so happy you are home safe."

I told Mama my plans to someday repay the kindness of those who helped me. "But for now, Mama, I'm thinking to join the CCC. I heard they're enlisting right now. Not only can I make some money for the family, Mama, but I'll be doing something good for the country. For our State. But, it does mean leaving again."

I didn't know how Mama would take that news, especially with Pa being gone for another month, but she took it all right. She made me agree to wait at least another two weeks before leaving again, and I thought it was more than reasonable. In the meantime, I helped around the house, and found some extra paid chores in town.

I visited the school and though it was closed for summer, I knew sometimes I might catch some staff there. Sure enough, I run into my old teacher. She said I passed my grade, but I already figured that. I just wanted to be sure to tell her why I left, and how all the things she taught me come flooding back to memory when I seen the country like I did. She was pleased and told me how teachers don't always get to know how their students make out in life. It made her feel good.

I also tried to get down to the barbershop, and spent an hour each afternoon listening to the old men tell their tales, nodding at some and debunking others. After all, I been out there. I'm a seasoned traveler now and I weren't as gullible. But they still made me laugh, and I tried hard to hold onto my imagination.

***

Those two weeks went by mighty fast and it come time, too soon, to pack a satchel for the CCC camp. Mama packed me up some of her canned goods, some bread and boiled eggs.

"Eat the things that'll spoil first, Billy," she said.

"I will, Mama, but they are gonna feed me, you know. And don't forget, they will be sending you a check for my work, and it is all yours for the house, you understand. I don't want you saving it aside for me—promise. I mean, they do it that way so you have something, and I get a little spending cash, too."

I knew she didn't like promising, but she did, and I give her back the nine dollars I brung home the week before. She had tried hiding it in my satchel—just like I knew she would.

"And this too, Mama," I said, sliding it back into her hand. "It's time for me to help out now."

Mama wanted to walk me into town to catch the bus. I was all registered with the government and ready. She put on her good straw hat, the one she kept just for church, and of course I wore my new trousers and shirt from Mrs. Willis, and my shoes. We waited for the bus outside the post office with a few other fellas—some I knew, some I didn't.

I never seen a tear in Mama's eye that day, and I didn't shed none, neither, as we both knew this was a good opportunity for her and for me. Mama kissed my cheek and I didn't mind, not even with the other fellas watching. She primped on me, smoothing down my hair, and I let her. That moment was for her, not for me.

"Blue! Hey, Blue!"

The man who run the post office come out just as I was about to step up into the bus.

"This come for you. It's from Washington!"

I thanked him as I took the letter, then I said goodbye to Mama. Really, I was so concentrated on saying goodbye, it didn't strike me until I was loaded and in my seat that I had a letter. I was waving at Mama when I glanced down at the envelope. It had the official stamp of the White House for a return address.

"The White House!" I threw open the window and leaned out. "Mama! It's from the White House!"

She couldn't hear what I said, as the bus pulled away. Mama was waving, and so was other folks, seeing off their sons and husbands.

I sat back in my seat, a bit stunned. *Well, I'll be doggone, I have a letter from the White House.*

I took out Pete's watch, turned it over, and read the inscription, "Veni vidi vici." Sure felt really right. *I came, I saw, I conquered.* Yessir, I did just fine.

As the bus rolled down the bumpy road outside town and crossed the tracks, I opened my letter and begun to read.

Dear Mr. *Saxton . . .* and again. *Dear* <u>Mr.</u> *Saxton . . .*

About the Author

As a storyteller, Lorna MacDonald Czarnota has delighted audiences in schools, libraries, festivals and conferences throughout the United States, Canada, and Ireland with traditional and original stories since 1985. Lorna specializes in original tales, adaptation of classic fairy tales often with music, Celtic, historical and healing story. Her historical presentations include Colonial America, Medieval, American Civil war, and the Dust Bowl. Lorna sang Depression era songs with the Blue Eagle String Band.

She is the author of *Wicked Niagara: the Sinister Side of the Niagara Frontier*; *Legends, Lore and Secrets of Western New York*; *Medieval Tales That Kids Can Read and Tell*; "One Lace Glove"; *August House Book of Scary Stories*; "The Bleeding Heart"; *The Healing Heart Community.*

Lorna is a member of the Society for Children's Book Writers and Illustrators, and The National Storytelling Network.

Lorna is a recipient of the Oracle Award from the National Storytelling Network, the Hopevale Incorporated Volunteer of the Year Award, Storytelling World Award, and was nominated as a Univera, United Way Community Hero.

A classroom guide is available for this book. Please contact the author.

Website: Storyhavenstudio.com or Lornamacdonaldczarnota.com

Phone: (716) 837-0551

email: Lczarnota@aol.com

Lorna MacDonald Czarnota specializes in work with at-risk youth through story. Her book *Dancing at the Crossroads: Mentoring At-Risk Youth through Story* is forthcoming with Parkhurst Brothers, Inc.

Also watch for *Pioneer Settlements and Native American Sites of New York State routes 5&20*, from History Press.

CPSIA information can be obtained at www.ICGtesting.com
Printed in the USA
BVOW080815140313

315507BV00001B/1/P

9 781939 289117